A flicker r.

Beside her, Garrett reached for his gun. "Stay here," he commanded. "Someone tried to kill you today. He could be back to finish the job." He pushed open her front door and entered the house.

But she wasn't going to obey his command. Her son was inside that house!

"Jacob!" She ran past Garrett and inside.

"Ashlynn, wait."

Sounds from the TV greeted her, but she heard nothing else. The house was too quiet. Panic ripped through her and she searched in a haze of anxiety and fear...but he wasn't anywhere to be seen.

"Jacob!"

She rushed into the next room and tripped over something. A leg jutting out from behind the couch. The nanny. Ashlynn didn't need to check for a pulse to know she was dead.

Garrett grabbed her shoulders and she sank into his arms. The nanny was dead, murdered, and Jacob... If something had happened to him...

Anguish rushed through her.

Where was her child?

Virginia Vaughan is a born-and-raised Mississippi girl. She is blessed to come from a large Southern family, and her fondest memories include listening to stories recounted around the dinner table. She was a lover of books from a young age, devouring tales of romance, danger and love. She soon started writing them herself. You can connect with Virginia through her website, virginiavaughanonline.com, or through the publisher.

Books by Virginia Vaughan

Love Inspired Suspense

Rangers Under Fire

Yuletide Abduction
Reunion Mission
Ranch Refuge
Mistletoe Reunion Threat

No Safe Haven

MISTLETOE REUNION THREAT

VIRGINIA VAUGHAN

HARLEQUIN® LOVE INSPIRED® SUSPENSE

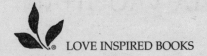

Recycling programs
for this product may
not exist in your area.

LOVE INSPIRED BOOKS

ISBN-13: 978-0-373-44787-9

Mistletoe Reunion Threat

Copyright © 2016 by Virginia Vaughan

www.Harlequin.com

Printed in U.S.A.

He has watched over your journey through this vast desert. These forty years the Lord your God has been with you, and you have not lacked anything.
—Deuteronomy 2:7

This book is lovingly dedicated to my family. Thank you all for putting up with me during this incredible journey. You know me at my best and at my worst and still love me.

ONE

Assistant District Attorney Ashlynn Morris's hands were shaking as she hurried down the steps of the courthouse toward her car. It couldn't be him. It just couldn't. But it had been Garrett Lewis in the foyer of the courthouse. The one man she'd never expected to see again.

She hadn't seen him in years—five to be exact—and she hadn't allowed herself to think about him in all that time except when she looked into her son Jacob's face and saw Garrett's eyes staring back at her. But she wouldn't give him the satisfaction of knowing how he'd devastated her when he abruptly ended their engagement, choosing his life as an army ranger over a life with her and Jacob.

The December wind nipped at her cheeks as she reached her car and opened the door, dumping belongings that had been in her briefcase onto the seat. She hadn't even bothered to slip on her coat in her haste to get out of the courthouse. She'd gone stone cold when she'd seen Garrett standing in the hall, his hands casually in his pockets and his easygoing manner apparent. His sandy hair was long on his neck and ears, and a goatee decorated his face, but his eyes were unmistakably kind when he turned to look at her, his expression just as surprised as she knew her own must be. She'd frozen in place, engulfed in a trance until someone had bumped into her, knocking her briefcase from her hands and spilling its contents on the floor. After quickly recovering her items with the stranger's help, she'd turned and rushed from the courthouse.

"Ashlynn," Garrett called, his baritone voice another shock to her system. "Ashlynn, wait."

How could she face him now when she'd loved him so amazingly deeply? He'd shattered her world by rejecting her, leaving her a twenty-two-year-old law school student suddenly on her own with a baby on the way.

It had been a struggle to raise a child alone and finish law school, but she hadn't given up. She'd fought for a better life for herself and Jacob just as she'd battled for everything good in her life. Her mentor, Judge Warren, often called her a survivor, and she was. She handled more pressure on a daily basis in her job as a prosecutor than most people ever faced, and she never blinked. She wouldn't—she couldn't—let Garrett see her blink, either.

Steeling herself against the emotions that threatened to overwhelm her, she shut her car door quickly before she acted on her need to jump inside and roar away. She would face him. It was time to finally put this behind her once and for all. Tucking her hair behind her ear, she took a deep, fortifying breath then turned and closed the distance between them. "Garrett, what are you doing here?"

His green eyes bored into hers so intensely that it made her breath catch, and when he spoke, his low, husky voice was just as she remembered; his deep southern drawl unmistakable. "I've started mentoring foster kids through my local church, and one of the boys is here to see his mother, who was picked up for drugs. I'm here to support him."

Her mind spun at the idea that he was mentoring foster kids. Yes, he'd been one, and yes, he'd found a successful career as an army ranger, but what kind of role model ran out on the people who needed him most? He might fool some with his good-guy act, but not her, not after how he'd abandoned her. But he'd misunderstood her question. "No, what are you doing here in Jackson?"

"Oh, that. I've been back in town for a while now. I'm living over on Sutton Lane out by the Reservoir." He gave her an uncertain shrug. "I didn't know whether or not to call. I heard you'd gotten married and started a family."

Yes, she'd gone on with her life after he'd left her. No need for him to know how it was currently falling apart. Her marriage was over, and her ex-husband wanted Jacob to live with him full-time. But those were her problems, and he didn't need to know about them.

"It's better you didn't," she said, determined not to let her vulnerability show. "We've both moved on."

"I'm working with the police now. I took a job training local law enforcement in anti-terror response tactics."

She gasped at this revelation. "You left the army?" Being a ranger had been everything to him. He'd chosen that life over a life with her, having promised to marry her during an extended leave from the rangers only to change his mind once he rejoined his unit.

He nodded, but his voice caught and she thought she spotted something lurking in his eyes—pain? "I did."

For Ashlynn, that was a final blow to her ego. He'd told her he couldn't be a ranger and be with her, then he'd abandoned them both. Now he would be around town and working with the police. She might see him through the course of her work. Jackson, Mississippi, was a big town, but law enforcement was a small community, and in her job as a prosecutor she often worked closely with the police. It was just one more insulting kick in the teeth to her already encumbered life. "I have to go. I'm expected at home."

She hurried away from him and back toward her car. It unnerved her to think he was so close now and she might see him regularly. She made a mental note to conduct as much of her business as possible at the secondary jailhouse, where she would be less likely to run into him again instead of the primary jailhouse where he was now working. But, for now, she needed to concentrate on Jacob and looked forward to winding down after an incredibly hectic day by snuggling with him on the couch tonight and watching *A Charlie Brown Christmas* on television.

She was nearly to her car when an explosion rocked

the air. Ashlynn was thrown backward, landing hard on the asphalt. She tumbled back against a car, ramming her head. Blinding pain ripped through her and her head felt heavy, but she managed to glance up to see her car in flames and debris falling all around. People were running toward her. Garrett was the only one she could make out clearly. He appeared to be screaming, but she couldn't hear him or anything over the ringing in her ears.

He reached her and pulled her to her feet then hurried her away from the debris and flames. Her body was numb, but when her knees buckled beneath her, he scooped her into his arms and carried her. Noise began to seep back through to her—the huff of air through Garrett's lungs as he ran, the distant wail of sirens and the roar of the fire raging a few feet away. The overwhelming smell of burning rubber permeated the air. She caught the worried expression on Garrett's face as her vision faded, and she laid her head against his chest and slipped into unconsciousness.

The sky was on fire from the force of the blast and the heat radiating from what was left of the car. As she passed out in his arms, a horrible realization rushed through Garrett. He'd seen her put her things into the vehicle that was now ablaze. That was definitely her car. A sickening feeling pulsed through him. If he hadn't stopped her, she would have been inside the car when it had blown up.

The explosion immediately made him think of his time in the army and the night his ranger team was ambushed. Five years later and he was still reliving it. Anything could bring those memories front and center again, whisking him back to that dark place. To the echoing blasts of mortars and gunfire, the cries of agony and the anguish of hauling his best friend from the battle only to have him die in Garrett's arms. This was his Ashlynn in the line of fire. And here he was, carrying someone he cared for out of danger once again. The way she slumped in his arms filled him with terror.

Please, God, don't let her be seriously injured.

People rushed from the courthouse and surrounding downtown buildings. The fire still raged and the air smelled putrid. He carefully set Ashlynn down in a patch of grass beside the courthouse steps. She was light as a feather in his arms, and her skin was soft as he touched her face. Her brown hair spilled from a clip at the back of her neck. And he'd noticed while they were talking that her eyes still blazed with fire and her chin jutted when she spoke. She was a petite powerhouse of dedication and energy when she fixated on something important to her. He'd always loved that about her.

He turned back to look at the car. Black smoke was pouring from it. He'd broken their engagement five years ago in order to keep her safe. His job as an army ranger had been a dangerous one, something he hadn't fully considered in the midst of their whirlwind courtship. But on returning to the army after proposing, he had, in fact, been scarred by war and the ambush that wiped out his ranger squad.

It was that ambush, and watching his friends die

and turn their wives into widows and their kids into orphans, that had convinced him he didn't want that life for Ashlynn. He hadn't wanted to saddle her with wondering if he would come home from a mission. He was glad she'd gotten on with her life, glad she'd found someone else to love and start a family with. Yet he'd always assumed her life without him would be quiet and uneventful. He'd never once dreamed she might become the victim of a car bomb.

The police arrived from the downtown precinct behind the courthouse. He could see the confusion on their faces as they wondered what had happened. Their first priority would be to keep the public safely away from the blaze and then scope out the area for other threats of danger.

He spotted his friend Vince Mason, his liaison with the Jackson police department, and called to him.

"What happened?" Vince asked, running up to him. "Did you see?"

Garrett swallowed the lump forming in his throat. "It was a car bomb."

"Do we know whose car it was?"

Again Garrett held the answer. He glanced at Ashlynn lying unconscious on the grass. "It was hers."

Vince stepped around him and saw her on the grass. "An attack on an ADA? That's not good. How is she?"

"She needs medical attention."

"Paramedics are on the way. Stay with her. We're going to have to question you about what you saw," he said, hurrying away. "Don't go anywhere."

He needn't have worried. Garrett wasn't leaving, not

until he knew Ashlynn was all right. It had been her dream to become a lawyer and then a prosecutor ever since Judge Warren had encouraged her pursuit of law after her testimony against her abusive foster mother helped send the woman to jail. He was proud of her for accomplishing her dreams, but he'd never considered the danger such a job might place her in.

What else had changed in her world, he wondered. Had she found God since their time together? He hoped she had. His newfound faith was the only thing that had sustained him through the past years since the ambush. And while he still struggled, he was thankful to have God on his side. He hoped Ashlynn had found the same comfort in Jesus that he had, especially when he realized how close she'd just come to meeting Him.

Ashlynn began to squirm. Her hand went to her head and she groaned. "What happened?"

He knelt beside her, in his heart a mix of relief that she seemed okay and horror over what had happened. "There was an explosion. How do you feel?"

She sat up and looked at him, her expression confused as if she didn't remember why he was there. She glanced past him toward the flames. The fire department had arrived on scene and was working to contain the blaze while the police were keeping people back, questioning witnesses and searching for other explosives. "My car."

"It could have been worse," he stated. "You could have been in it."

Again that thought sent shivers through him. He took a deep breath and thanked God for His intervention today in keeping Ashlynn safe. Garrett had let her go five years ago in order to keep her safe.

Yet it seemed she'd managed to find danger all on her own.

Ashlynn allowed the paramedics to check her out and bandage a few scrapes she'd sustained in the explosion, but she waved off any talk of going to the hospital. She wasn't seriously injured and she needed to get home to be with her son and relieve her nanny, Mira. Her mind was scrambled by the thought that someone had tried to kill her. Who had placed that bomb in her car? And why? She didn't know, but the idea that someone might want her dead shook her.

Garrett approached with the precinct commander and Ashlynn realized that seeing Garrett again after all this time had shaken her nearly as much as the threat against her life. At first, she'd thought he was a dream or a flashback when she'd opened her eyes and seen him hovering over her, but then the events of the afternoon had come rushing in. Garrett Lewis was back in her life.

"Ashlynn, this is Vince Mason, he's—"

"I know who he is," she insisted, suddenly irritated that he thought he could waltz into town and act like she was the outsider. "I work with this police force every day." She'd struggled to put herself through law school after Garrett left her, and she had been working in the DA's office for nearly two years now.

Vince nodded. "Yes, we've worked together on cases many times. How are you feeling, counselor?"

Her ears were still ringing and she was sore, but mostly she was ready to wrap her son in a big hug. "I'm fine. I'm anxious to get home."

"I know you are. I need to ask you some questions first, though. Do you have any idea who would place a bomb on your car?"

"Not at all." It was the truth. She hadn't worked any high-profile cases during her time in the DA's office. In fact, she hadn't worked any cases she could remember involving explosives of any kind.

"Have you received any threats recently?"

"No."

"Can you think of anyone, perhaps someone you prosecuted, who would want to do you harm? We can check on people you've convicted that might have recently been released from prison or escaped."

"I don't make a lot of friends in my job as a prosecutor, but no one has made overt threats. I can have my investigator send you some names to check out. He's familiar with all the threats the office receives."

He nodded. "Tell him to call me. Meanwhile, I'm going to follow up with forensics to see if there's any identifying information about that bomb. Fortunately, we haven't discovered any further devices. Until we determine otherwise, it appears you were the primary target. Would you like me to have an officer drive you home?"

"Yes, that would be good," Ashlynn said. She couldn't wait to go home and wash this day from her memory.

"No need. I'll take her," Garrett said.

Vince looked at her questioningly, allowing her to make the decision.

"It's fine," she said, and Vince nodded.

"I'll be in touch, then." He walked off, leaving Ashlynn alone with Garrett as he hurried back to the scene.

"You didn't have to offer," she said. She didn't want him thinking she couldn't take care of herself. She was a successful career woman. She'd built a life without him.

But the glint of his smile melted her resolve. "I would feel better knowing you made it home safely. Besides, I don't mind."

She hated that he could still have such an effect on her, but she'd been captivated by Garrett ever since he first smiled at her at a friend's party. She'd been fresh out of college and he was already a decorated soldier home on an extended leave. She'd fallen hard and fast, and his protective manner had made her feel safe and loved for the first time in her life. But she wasn't that young girl anymore and she didn't need rescuing...yet she did like the way his hand rested protectively on the small of her back, guiding her and keeping her steady as they walked toward his truck.

He opened the door for her to sit in the passenger's seat then walked around and slid behind the wheel. He grinned at her in a familiar manner she remembered so well, and she felt her heart flutter. Maybe this wasn't such a good idea. She'd just wanted to get home. But now, the twenty-minute drive to her neighborhood seemed like an eternity. What did one say to the man who'd promised to spend his life with her then left her and her unborn child to pursue his career as a ranger?

After giving him directions to her home, she decided avoiding anything personal was the best solution. She should call Ken Barrett, her investigator at the DA's office, and get him started on gathering those names for Vince. But her phone was a charred mess in what was left of her car. "May I borrow your cell phone to call my investigator?" Her first task tomorrow would be obtaining a new phone.

He handed it over and she dialed Ken's number, thankful she knew it by heart. He answered, his deep bass voice familiar and reassuring. She had only known him six months, but they had become fast friends in that time, and she often looked to him as a brotherly figure, though they were only ten years apart in age.

"Ashlynn? Are you okay? I heard about what happened downtown. Is it true someone placed a bomb in your car?"

"It does look that way," she admitted. "Vince Mason wants a list of all the threats our office has received, especially any directed at me specifically or any involving explosive devices."

"I'll take care of it," he said, then in a tone of concern added, "I'm glad you're safe. I wish you'd be more careful, Ashlynn. I've tried to warn you that there are a bunch of crazies out there."

"I know, Ken, but I'm fine. I just want to get home. I'll see you tomorrow at the office."

She ended the call, then handed the phone back to Garrett. He slid it into a holder on the dashboard. Suddenly, the silence grew awkward between them, and she realized she should have kept Ken on the phone longer. She could have asked him for an update on any number of cases they were working on together.

The uncomfortable silence lengthened. At least they were nearly to her house.

"So, you have a son," he said. "What's his name?"

Her heart hammered in her chest at his question. She didn't like where this conversation was going. Didn't want him asking about Jacob. He'd given up that right when he'd abandoned them, and she already had one man trying to pull her child from her. She didn't need another. She had to keep him at arm's length when it came to her little boy. How could he ever make up for the fact that he hadn't wanted her and his child?

"Jacob," she said, then thankfully noticed they were nearing her home. "That's my house," she said, pointing out the driveway. He pulled in and parked beside Mira's small sedan.

"Thank you for the ride," she said, hoping that would be the end of it and they could each go their separate ways.

But Garrett was already getting out. "I'd feel better if you let me check inside."

"That's really not necessary."

"Someone tried to kill you today, Ashlynn. Who's to say they haven't come here to finish the job?"

"I would know if someone had been here, Garrett. I have a security system."

He spotted the car in the driveway. "I guess your husband would have phoned you, huh?"

It was none of his business about her marriage, and she didn't want him to think she'd failed without him.

"My nanny and son are in the house. Mira would have called me if something was wrong."

"Still, I would feel better if you'd let me check it out. It won't take long."

She finally relented and walked to the front door. Anything to satisfy him and get him away from her home and away from her son. However, she stopped walking when she noticed the front door ajar, a flicker of fear racing through her.

Garrett saw it too and stiffened as he reached for his gun, pushing past her. "Stay here," he commanded. He shoved open the door and entered the house.

But she wasn't going to obey that command. Her son was inside that house. If someone else was there, someone who meant to get back at her by harming her son, she wasn't going to be still.

"Jacob!" she screamed, hurrying past him and running up the stairs.

"Ashlynn, wait."

She heard his footsteps behind her but she wouldn't stop until she knew Jacob was safe.

Sounds from the TV in the playroom greeted her at the top of the stairs, but she heard nothing else. Jacob was a rambunctious four-year-old and the house was too quiet. Panic ripped through her and she took the last few stairs in a haze of anxiety and fear. She pushed open the playroom door. Jacob's toys littered the floor and the television was still playing his favorite evening show…but he wasn't anywhere to be seen.

"Jacob!"

She rushed into the room, intent on looking in his favorite hiding spots. She tripped over something beside the couch and hit the floor, landing hard on her hands. Ashlynn turned to see what she'd tripped over and saw a leg jutting out from behind the couch. Panic hit her at the sight. It was too big to be Jacob's leg, but...

She looked up at Garrett, who now stood in the doorway, his gun drawn. His eyes focused on the leg. She moved to look behind the couch and saw Mira on the floor. The young girl wasn't moving, her eyes were vacant, and the carpet was stained red with blood around her.

Ashlynn didn't need to check for a pulse to know Mira was dead.

She screamed Jacob's name and leaped to her feet. If someone had broken in and killed Mira, Jacob might have gotten scared and hidden.

"Jacob!" She ran down the hall to his bedroom and burst in, searching under the bed and in the closet. He wasn't there. She checked her bedroom then rushed downstairs. She called for him, frantic with worry as she checked every nook and cubby, searching for any place he might have hidden.

He was nowhere to be found.

Panic filled her. Mira was dead, murdered, and Jacob was missing. If something had happened to him...

Ashlynn dropped to her knees as anguish rushed through her.

Where was her child? *Oh, God, where is Jacob?*

Seeing her this way was like a sucker punch to his gut, and all Garrett wanted to do was sweep her up into his arms and make everything better. He checked that response, realizing not only might she object, but her husband wouldn't be too thrilled with him, either. He'd noticed the family portrait of them when he entered the house. And he no longer had that right. Even if she hadn't been married with a child, there could never be a future for them, not after all he'd seen and all he'd done. He'd walked out of a firefight unscathed when other men, better men with families, had died, and his grief had pushed him to kill and maim all in the name of war.

But his heart hurt for her. He couldn't imagine the devastation of having her child ripped from her. She'd already had such a difficult life, having lost her parents in a car accident when she was eight then being placed in an abusive foster home and nearly beaten to death by her foster mother. But it seemed she'd turned that all around now. She had a nice home in a fancy neighborhood, a good job in the DA's office and a beautiful family.

He holstered his gun and pulled out his cell phone to alert the police about the dead girl in the playroom and the missing child. This couldn't be a coincidence. It had to somehow be connected to the bomb in her car earlier today.

Garrett stopped dialing when he heard a noise from outside the house. His ears perked up and all his senses went on alert. He put away his phone and retrieved his gun. Someone was here. He grabbed Ashlynn's hand, pulled her to her feet and pressed his hand against her mouth to keep her from speaking. Her eyes widened in fear and her lashes were wet with tears, but she didn't ask questions.

"Follow me," he whispered, his instincts warning him to tread cautiously. He led her away from the front windows but peered out of them from the side, peeking through the heavy curtains. He saw nothing but the setting sun.

Something was wrong. He felt it in his gut. He sensed someone watching them. His truck was parked in the driveway but the direct route to it would be dangerous if he was right and someone was out there.

He grabbed a lamp from the end table and waggled it in front of the window. A shot rang out, bursting through the glass and shattering the lamp in his hand. Ashlynn screamed, but Garrett grabbed her arm and pulled her back up the stairs, his heart heavy at the continuing threat against her. Now that the shooter had made himself known, but failed to kill them, he would watch the exits closely or possibly come inside to finish them off. They had to find a way out of the house.

He led her into the master bedroom and locked the door. It wouldn't hold off an intruder with a gun for long, but possibly long enough for them to escape. He had his weapon, but it would be no match for the shooter's gun which, by the sound of it, Garrett recognized as a semi-automatic rifle, a serious weapon with serious intent. He hurried to the balcony and swung open the doors. Their only chance was to get out of this house, and now that they were upstairs this was their only way out. They would have to jump. He glanced down and saw a concrete patio below. It wasn't a high drop, but it would hurt. He holstered his gun.

"I'll go first. Then you follow behind me."

She shook her head, fear pooling in her wide brown eyes. "I can't."

"You have to, Ashlynn. You have to stay alive for Jacob." His words were meant to provoke her to action, knowing she would do whatever she had to in order to find her son. It worked. She considered his words for only a moment before fortifying herself and nodding.

He crawled over the railing and climbed down, letting himself drop and hitting the ground. Pain ripped through his leg, but he ignored it. He'd sustained worse injuries and kept moving. He looked up and motioned for Ashlynn to jump.

She nodded and swung one leg over the railing. Just then, he heard the sound of the door cracking open and the shout of the gunman as he burst into the room. Ashlynn's head jerked up and the *dat-dat-dat* of gunfire filled the air. His gut clenched as her fingers slipped from the railing and she fell, tumbling backward toward the ground.

TWO

She felt herself falling, and her only thoughts were of Jacob and to wonder if he was crying for her. She was going to die without ever knowing what had happened to him.

She slammed into something hard and felt Garrett's arms surround her as they both fell to the ground. He scrambled up before she could even process what was happening and pulled them both toward the safety of the house as the shooter fired over the balcony. Garrett's arm tightened protectively around her and Ashlynn was surprised by the way her heart picked up speed at being this close to him. She chided herself. Her son was missing and someone was shooting at her, but she felt safe swept up in his arms.

Garrett pulled his gun and fired upward into the balcony. Tension was rolling off him in waves. The shooter scrambled back into the room to avoid the shots.

"Run to my truck now," Garrett commanded, and Ashlynn did as she was told without question. She heard shots and screamed at the fear that ripped through her, but she didn't stop running. She was also keenly aware that Garrett was beside her, matching her steps and stopping every now and then to return fire into her house before easily catching up with her. The Christmas lights she'd placed on a timer flickered on, illuminating her bullet-riddled home and making this entire situation seem less real and more like a terrible action movie gone wrong.

She reached the pickup and slid into the passenger's seat. He jumped behind the wheel and started the engine, roaring away a moment later. The shooter started firing again and shots hit the vehicle. One pinged the rear windshield, causing it to shatter. Ashlynn winced as glass spilled over her but she knew it could have been so much worse.

She glanced in the side mirror and saw a masked man with a long gun run toward a waiting car.

"Hang on," Garrett said, then punched down on the accelerator, putting distance between them and the man, their attacker.

Ashlynn was shivering by the time they reached the downtown police precinct and it wasn't from the chill in the December air. Whoever had been shooting at them either hadn't been able to keep up with Garrett's driving or had given up. It didn't matter if they didn't kill her right then. They had her son, which meant they could have whatever they wanted from her. She would do anything to get him back.

Garrett led her inside, telling the on-duty officer

about the incident. Within minutes, the precinct was on alert.

Garrett slipped his jacket around her shoulders and tried to offer her comfort as he led her to a quiet office. "They've got officers headed to your house right now to process the scene. They're also trying to contact your husband. Is it possible Jacob is with him?"

She saw a hopeful look in his expression, but she knew that wasn't the case and shook her head. "Mira doesn't live with us. If Stephen had picked up Jacob, she would have gone home."

"You don't live together?" Garrett asked, surprise coloring his face.

She shook her head. "He lives on Barrister Avenue in the Wood Hills subdivision. We divorced a few months ago." She didn't want to discuss such personal matters with Garrett, and thankfully, he didn't ask any further questions about her and Stephen. It was embarrassing to admit to him that her marriage had broken down.

Ashlynn felt numb. Her thoughts were all about Jacob. Her arms ached at the thought of not being able to hold him and her heart broke at the idea that he was probably crying for her. It wasn't fair! Ripping a child from his mother's arms was the cruelest thing anyone could do.

She'd never been much of a praying woman. Her anger at God was too strong. He had allowed too many bad things to come into her life. She'd foolishly thought things were turning around when she'd met Garrett, but then he'd turned against her, too, choosing the rangers over her and Jacob. And now it seemed God was still not on her side.

Vince arrived at the station, his hair tousled and his clothes dirty. Since she'd known him, he'd always been cool under pressure and presented a well-kept appearance. It was the first time she could remember seeing him look so disheveled. He apologized for not being there when they'd arrived and explained he'd had to leave to fix his wife's car that had stalled on the interstate. Garrett filled him in on what had happened, how they'd entered the house and found Mira dead, then been attacked by an armed gunman.

"Did you see the man?" Vince asked her once Garrett told him about the incident on the balcony. "Can you describe him?"

She thought back, reliving the terror of the man bursting into the room and raising his gun at her. But she wasn't able to offer much in the way of description. "He was wearing a dark mask over his face, like a ski mask, and he was dressed all in black. I couldn't see any of his features, but he was a large man, tall with big shoulders."

"He had an automatic weapon," Garrett added. "I would say by his tactics he's probably had some military experience. He came prepared."

Vince nodded. "The question is, did he come prepared to take the child or was it an impromptu decision? And why kill the nanny if Ashlynn is the one he wants?"

"We didn't see Jacob, but he could have had him tied up in the car."

Vince's face grew grim. "Whoever this guy is, he has access to both automatic weapons and explosives."

Ashlynn shuddered and folded her arms around her. They were talking so clinically, as if it wasn't her child missing or her world falling apart.

"Did Mira have any family that needs to be notified?" Vince asked her.

Ashlynn nodded. "Her parents live in Memphis."

"Is it possible this is about her?" Garrett asked.

"It's possible, but unlikely given the bomb was in Ashlynn's car." Vince looked at her. "What about your husband? I understand you divorced recently. Was it an amicable split?"

Ashlynn swallowed hard and wished Garrett wasn't listening to every word she said. She didn't like sharing information about her personal life, especially unpleasant details. She nodded. She doubted Stephen was involved in this. He was a good man and loved Jacob like his own son. "Stephen isn't a violent person. I can't believe he would try to kill me."

"But he could have hired someone to do it. It wouldn't be the first time a man has tried to off his ex-wife over a custody dispute. I'll send someone to his house to update him on what's happened and try to ascertain his involvement, if any." Vince's phone rang and he pulled it out. "It's the commander on scene at your house." He answered the call and listened intently.

Garrett walked over to her and rubbed her arms. "How are you holding up?"

She wanted to scream and rant, but her arms and legs were numb with shock and fear. Her chin trembled as she spoke. "I just want him back," she whispered, fighting with everything she had to keep her emotions under control. Falling apart now wouldn't do any good. She had to keep her wits about her in order to figure out who was targeting her and who had Jacob.

Vince ended his call and turned back to them.

"My men have been through the house and there's no sign of your son. We did gather photos of him." He pulled up one that had been sent to him. "Is this a recent snapshot?"

She looked at the photo and bit back tears. It was his preschool Christmas photo, taken only two weeks earlier. She traced the outline of his face, her heart breaking at the sight of his beautiful green eyes and his wide, mischievous smile. "Yes, it's very recent."

He nodded. "We'll add this photo to our Amber Alert. Don't worry, Ashlynn. We'll find him. Ken sent me those names and my officers are checking them all."

"How sure are you that this has to be someone she's prosecuted?" Garrett asked.

"Without any other identifiable enemies, it's a logical place to start. We're still on the scene processing the house and interviewing neighbors so we may find some more evidence that might lead us in the right direction there." He looked at her and his face softened. "You can't go home. Do you have somewhere to go, Ashlynn? Somewhere safe?"

"I'm not going anywhere until Jacob is found."

"You won't do anybody any good here. You need to get some rest."

"I can't rest until I know he's safe. Besides, with

someone trying to kill me, I couldn't possibly put any of my friends in danger that way."

Garrett placed an arm on her back, but he addressed Vince when he spoke. "She can come home with me. I'll keep her safe."

"No!" Ashlynn insisted. "I said I'm not leaving."

"I need you to rest, Ashlynn," Vince told her and Garrett agreed.

"You can't do Jacob any good if you're so tired you can't function. There's nothing you can do here."

She wanted to lash out at him for using Jacob against her. He had no right to act so concerned. He'd lost that right when he'd abandoned them five years ago. Yet she knew he was right. She needed to be at her best for Jacob's sake.

She stared up into Garrett's face and saw the worry in his expression. He wanted her to trust him and she instinctively desired to. She'd trusted him with everything she'd had once upon a time He'd been her rock and her protector, and she had to admit she was glad he was by her side now. Her initial displeasure at seeing him was beginning to fade. What would she have done if he hadn't been there? She would have been dead in her car this afternoon or at the very least in her house tonight.

But how could she rest when her child's life was at stake? She shuddered thinking of the possibility that Jacob might need her and she wasn't close by. She shook her head stubbornly. "I'm not going anywhere."

Garrett glanced over at Vince then tried a different tactic. "Okay then, we won't go anywhere. We'll stick around and man the phones for the Amber Alert." He looked at Vince, who nodded his agreement.

"I'll keep you updated if we get any new leads," he promised then walked off.

She was glad that was settled. She wasn't just any crime victim. She was also a prosecutor and she didn't want to be handled. She had to stay strong and make certain every lead and angle was being investigated in finding her son.

Garrett reached out and placed a reassuring hand on her arm that sent tingles through her. "We'll find him. I promise." She stared into his green eyes and melted a little inside, remembering how much she'd once loved this man. "Do you trust me, Ash?" he asked, using his old nickname for her.

She stared at her hands to avoid looking into his eyes. Every instinct told her she could trust him, but her heart knew better. She'd once trusted him more than anyone in the world. She'd believed he was someone she could count on forever, but that trust had ended when he'd shut them out after discovering she was pregnant. The memory of how alone and broken she'd been brought back anger and bitterness so intense that she nearly couldn't breathe.

Instead of answering him, she asked a question. "When did you leave the rangers?"

He looked like he didn't want to answer, but he did. "Two years ago."

So he'd given up on them for something he hadn't even stayed with.

He sighed. "I owe you an apology, Ash."

"No, you don't."

"Yes, I do, and I want to explain. I never told you this, but after I left you to return to my unit, my ranger team was ambushed. I saw men with wives and families who were suffering because their husbands and fathers had decided to take on a dangerous task. I knew I couldn't let you have that kind of life. My life, my work, is dangerous. I was trying to protect you from that."

She cut him off, anger pulsing through her at the idea that he was going to try to justify abandoning his family. "What you did was to make the choice for me. You made a decision that affected us without even consulting me. You cut me out of your life."

His expression held regret and pain, but he nodded reluctantly. "I know."

"I can't even begin to fathom how I can trust you to help me look for Jacob."

"I know I've let you down in the past, Ash, but I'm here now and I won't leave you again. I'm right here by your side and I promise you I'll find your son."

His eyes steeled with determination, but she noticed he still referred to Jacob as *her* son, not *their* son. Well, he was right. Jacob was her son. He'd abandoned them when they'd needed him most. But he had skills that could help her. He had been an army ranger. She needed him in order to find Jacob. And even though she didn't want to, she instinctively trusted him in that regard.

Garrett hung around the precinct and kept an eye on Ashlynn. For the next few hours, she answered calls from the Amber Alert and he could see the devastation on her face when each lead proved unworthy. He agreed with Vince that she didn't need to be here in the center of all this. She needed to distance herself and allow others to field through the evidence. Yet he also knew she wasn't the type of person to sit around and wait for answers. Like him, she was action oriented. It was one of those things he'd once loved most about her. She'd never played the part of a victim no matter how many obstacles life threw at her. He knew she wouldn't now, either.

He had to admit he was feeling antsy himself. He needed to do something and his mind was focused on speaking with Ashlynn's ex-husband, Stephen Morris. He'd been surprised to learn of their divorce. It wasn't really his business, but this was Ashlynn they were talking about, and as far as he was concerned she was still his business.

Despite what she'd told Vince earlier, his stomach constricted as he realized the attempt on her life along with her son's abduction made much more sense when you added an angry ex-husband to the mix, especially since they had yet to receive a ransom call. Had Stephen hired someone to plant that bomb in Ashlynn's car? And was he behind the murder of their nanny? He wanted to believe such a thing would shock him, but unfortunately he'd seen too much and was no longer surprised by the depravity of the world. Both his time in the rangers and his private search-and-rescue missions had cemented his belief that evil knew no bounds and betrayal was a bitter pill. It pained him to think that Ashlynn might have been betrayed by someone she'd once cared for.

He tracked down the detective Vince had sent to interview Ashlynn's ex and asked him what his take was on Stephen Morris.

"The husband would automatically become a person of interest in an attack on his wife, but this guy seemed genuinely shocked at the nanny's death and understandably worried about his kid. We'll keep looking into his business dealings and financials, but my personal opinion is that he's not involved."

Garrett hoped the detective was correct, but it was hard to take the man's opinion at face value. He didn't know him that well and didn't yet trust his judgment. In fact, there wasn't anyone on the force he trusted that much yet. Garrett wanted to look into Stephen's eyes himself in order to know for sure he wasn't involved in this.

But he wasn't leaving Ashlynn alone. He found her refilling a cup of coffee in the break room and pulled her aside. Her face showed signs of weariness and her eyes were red and sad. He hated seeing her this way and had the sudden urge to take her in his arms. Instead, he dug his hands into his pockets before he acted on it.

"How are you holding up?"

She shook her head. "It's frustrating. The Amber Alert isn't generating much usable information. I feel like I should be out doing something, even if it's just driving around with my head out the window screaming Jacob's name."

He smiled at that image, but he agreed with her sentiment. They'd been at the precinct for hours. They both needed to be out doing something.

"I was thinking we should go talk with your ex-husband. I know the police have already questioned him, but he may say something to you that he wouldn't say to the police."

"I know Stephen is the most logical suspect given that the bomb was in my car, but I still have a hard time believing he would kill Mira."

"This may have nothing to do with him or he could be involved indirectly. What if someone is targeting his family to get back at him? We should check out every possibility."

He could see she was still hesitant to believe Stephen could be involved, but her urge to do something obviously won out because she agreed to go with him. She followed him outside and slid into the passenger seat of his truck. The back window was still out so he cranked up the heater to knock off the chill of the December night air.

He headed for the neighborhood where Stephen Morris now lived. Garrett knew it by reputation. It was an upscale area in a well-to-do part of town. Stephen obviously made a good living. Garrett didn't like the twinge of jealousy that nicked at him. He wasn't some poor kid from the wrong side of town anymore. He, too, made a good living and while his house might not be as large or grand as this one, it offered him all he needed.

He slowed as they approached the house and he memorized the layout as he passed it. The garage door was closed. All the window blinds were down. The house seemed dark, but Garrett noticed a faint light in the kitchen window. It wasn't unusual even this close to midnight, but it caught his attention. He scanned the area looking for suspicious cars or activity that might indicate that whoever was after Ashlynn had either followed them there or was waiting for them.

"That's his house," Ashlynn stated, pointing. "You just passed Stephen's house."

He sped up and turned, circling the block. "I know. I'm checking out the area first."

"Oh." She glanced out the windshield and tried to see something. "Do you see anything?"

"No. Everything looks clear." He wished they had stopped by his house first so he could grab his gun bag. The only weapon he had on him was the pistol he always carried. He didn't like to walk into any situation unprepared. Ashlynn didn't believe her ex could be involved, but Garrett had seen too many relationships go bad to take anything for granted. "I see a light coming from the side window. Looks like he might be up." But was he awake because he was hiding his son in the house or because he was concerned about the shooting gone wrong at his former home?

Garrett parked several houses down and got out. He placed his arm on her elbow as they approached the house. She headed for the front door, but he stopped her.

"We're not going in that way."

"Why not?"

"Ashlynn, we have to make sure he isn't in on this. I

want to know what's going on inside that house before we enter. If he's involved, he might have Jacob inside."

He moved quietly around the side until they reached the back. He glanced in through a window. The kitchen was dark except for a light above the sink, but Stephen Morris sat at the table poring over his laptop. Garrett pushed Ashlynn behind him then found a stick and used it to scratch against the back door. He watched Stephen react to the sound. Stephen stood and glanced out the window but Garrett pushed Ashlynn down so they wouldn't be seen. He heard the locks on the door unlatch and knew Stephen was coming out to investigate. Garrett readied his weapon and when the door opened, he leaped forward and pushed Stephen back into the house, his gun raised and aimed at the man's head. Stephen stumbled backward, his hands up in a surrendering manner until he saw Ashlynn enter behind Garrett.

She rushed past him and ran toward the bedrooms, calling her son's name. She reappeared several moments later, disappointment coloring her face. "He's not here."

Stephen's eyes rounded in surprise as he stared at her, then anger set in. "Of course he's not here. I wish he was. The police have already been here and filled me in on what's happened." His eyes bored into hers. "I knew working that job in the DA's office would bring nothing but trouble. It's already destroyed our marriage. Now it's taken our son."

"Did you have anything to do with that, Stephen?"

He sighed. "No, Ashlynn, of course not. How could you think I could be involved?"

Garrett motioned for Stephen to sit down at the table and he put away the gun. He pulled the laptop to him and examined the screen. Stephen Morris appeared to be looking up only investment statistics. It seemed an odd thing to focus on when your child was missing, but other than that it didn't strike him as a suspicious activity. Perhaps he was merely trying to keep his mind off his missing child.

It was looking more and more possible that he wasn't involved, and Garrett was glad. He would hate to believe Ashlynn had been betrayed again by someone she thought cared for her.

But then who had Jacob, and why?

Ashlynn sat down and her shoulders slumped, defeated. He knew she hadn't really thought her ex was involved, but it must be hitting her hard that Jacob wasn't here. At least if he'd been with his father, she would know he wasn't in any danger. She no longer had that assurance. The lack of a ransom request after all these hours didn't bode well for Jacob's safe homecoming. Kidnappers who didn't want a ransom generally had no intention of returning the child. That meant finding him soon became much more urgent for his safety.

Garrett faced Stephen Morris and got down to business. "Someone is targeting your ex-wife and son, Stephen. Family can be a powerful weapon to use against a person. What are you into?"

"I don't know what you are talking about. I'm not

into anything." Stephen grew a little more confident and gave Garrett a harsh look. "Who are you, anyway?"

"I'm an old friend of your wife's and I'm the one who is going to find out what's going on here."

Stephen looked at Ashlynn. "You have to believe me. I have no idea why someone would be doing this to us. It must have something to do with one of your cases."

She closed her eyes against his accusation. Garrett knew she was already worrying that her job could have made her son a target. She didn't need Stephen reminding her. A tear slipped from her eye. She wiped it away before rushing to the bathroom.

Garrett gave him a long, hard stare, not liking the accusation he'd hurled at Ashlynn. "The police are sifting through her files and following up on that. We're looking into different angles."

"I'm telling you I had nothing to do with this. I want to find Jacob and bring him home."

"Ashlynn told me you're suing for custody. If you thought you might lose, that's a good motive to have her killed."

Stephen shook his head. "I've already decided to drop that suit. I called my attorney this afternoon. I hoped Ashlynn and I could work this out between ourselves."

"That's convenient. You drop the custody suit and suddenly Jacob goes missing."

"I've already told you I had nothing to do with that. I would never hurt Jacob. I've helped raise him these

past three years. I love him like he's my own child."
He fidgeted uncomfortably in his chair but his words
had a feel of truth to them.

But one point struck Garrett as odd. "When you say
you love him like he's your own child, are you imply-
ing that Jacob isn't your biological son?"

Stephen nodded. "Jacob was already born when
Ashlynn and I got married, but that doesn't mean he's
not my son. He is."

Garrett looked toward the closed door where she'd
disappeared as a rush of thoughts flooded him. If it
was true that Ashlynn's ex wasn't the father of her
child...who was?

Ashlynn went to the bedroom Stephen had fixed up
for Jacob. The boy loved being here and Stephen was a
good father. She picked up one of the stuffed animals
on the bed and hugged it to herself. Where was Jacob
right now? She couldn't help wondering if he was safe.
Was he crying for her? Shame and guilt filled her. She
should have been there for him.

That's why her marriage had broken down, too. Stephen had told her she spent too much time worrying
about work and not about him. He'd called her obsessed
and maybe he was right.

She'd always hated the injustice of the world, mostly
because in her childhood she'd been a victim of life.
She'd made a vow to herself that she would provide a
better life for her child, and while she hadn't gotten off
to a good start—his own father hadn't wanted him—
she had mostly succeeded.

Jacob would never have to worry about the lights being turned off for lack of payment or going hungry because his father spent all their grocery money on booze. Yes, Stephen had been a good husband and father. He'd provided for them well, and still did. Yet she hadn't been able to keep it all together for him and he'd obviously sensed it and felt alienated. She'd never loved Stephen the way he'd wanted her to, and she knew the reason was standing in his kitchen right now.

The connection she'd shared with Garrett could never be topped. She'd done a disservice to Stephen by marrying him when she couldn't forget Garrett, but she'd done what she'd thought was best for her baby at the time. She'd given him the father who wanted him and could provide a good life for him. And she had loved Stephen and been hurt when he'd left her, although that pain had been nothing like she'd felt when Garrett walked away.

Indignation bristled through her at that reminder. She would never allow him to hurt Jacob. She may need him, even be grateful to him, for helping her find Jacob, but once her son was home safely, Garrett Lewis could not be a part of their lives.

Garrett scanned the living room, looking at photos that were all around. A large Christmas tree that looked flawlessly decorated stood in the corner. Not an ornament was out of place. It looked too picture-perfect for a house with a four-year-old and he doubted Stephen Morris had done the job himself. His gaze landed on the mantel and pictures depicting happier times with

Stephen, Ashlynn and Jacob—a trip to Niagara Falls, a photo in front of the Eiffel Tower, Jacob's second birthday party, complete with cake and candles and Billie the Bear, a franchise he recognized as a local favorite for kids.

He turned away from the photos. They were painful to look at. That should have been him with Ashlynn and only his foolishness had prevented it. Letting her go had been one of his greatest mistakes, but at the same time he knew it had been for the best. He hadn't been seriously injured in the ambush that took the lives of many of his friends, but it had shattered his life in ways he was still discovering.

Only Colton had escaped physically unscathed, although Garrett knew he'd carried emotional wounds deep inside him until he'd met Laura Jackson recently and found a reason to believe in life again. Garrett missed the times he and Colton had spent working together after leaving the rangers, just the two of them on privately funded search-and-rescue missions. After Colton had hung up his gear and retired to ranch life, the solitude had quickly turned to loneliness for Garrett.

That was when his friend and former Ranger buddy Josh Adams had heard about the opening at the local police agency and all his ranger friends had encouraged him to take the job. Garrett was glad he'd finally relented. He enjoyed the camaraderie with others and enjoyed putting his skills in action in a way that didn't always have to put his life in danger. Only a few days ago, he'd convinced himself he was content with his life now, but seeing Ashlynn, hearing her voice and having her need him, had sent him once again into a tailspin. And having evidence of her perfect life before him in high-quality photos didn't make it any easier. Ashlynn might now be single, but he'd done too much to ever be worthy of a woman like her.

"Are you him?" Stephen asked from the doorway, causing Garrett to startle. "Are you the one who broke her heart?"

Heat rose in his face as he realized Stephen Morris had just managed to sneak up on him, all because he'd had Ashlynn on his mind.

"She never got over it," Stephen continued. "I tried to make it work between us. I thought she would learn to love me the way I loved her, but that never happened. I just wish she could have—"

Suddenly, a shot rang out. Garrett ducked, reaching for his gun as he watched the bullet burst through the glass in the window and slam into Stephen's chest. The force of it knocked Stephen from his feet, tossing him backward. He landed on the edge of the sofa then slid to the floor, the life draining from him in a matter of moments.

THREE

Ashlynn ran into the room at the sound of the shot. She saw Stephen on the floor and called out his name, trying to reach him. Garrett grabbed her around the waist and threw her to the floor. Whoever had made that shot was still out there and Garrett was certain he or Ashlynn would be his next target.

Yet he also knew they couldn't stay here. The shooter would be coming inside soon to finish the job, just as he'd done at Ashlynn's house. Garrett considered their options. No way they would make it all the way to his truck without being seen. He slid across the floor to where Stephen lay motionless and searched through his pockets for his car keys. He hadn't seen Stephen's car in the driveway, so it had to be in the attached garage. If they could make it there, they might have a chance.

He reached for Ashlynn's hand. "We're going to the garage. Stay low and remain quiet."

She nodded her agreement then followed him, her hand pressing tightly into his. He had his gun in his other hand, but it wouldn't do much good against a long-range shooter. He'd have to get closer to do any real damage, but he could and would use it for cover fire if necessary. After all, whoever was shooting didn't know what kind of weapon he had on him.

He led Ashlynn through the kitchen to the garage entrance. There were no windows so they were able to stand normally in here. They rushed to the car and Garrett was glad to see it was a BMW. The higher quality German-made steel would be better able to withstand the gunshots that were sure to be fired at them and the engine was powerful enough to whisk them away quickly.

He slid behind the wheel while Ashlynn dived into the passenger seat, pulling on her seatbelt. He paused. Once he started the car, it was do or die for them. He glanced at Ashlynn to make sure she was ready. Her nod told him she was.

He lifted a silent prayer that they would make it through this, then hit the start button and pressed the automatic opener on the visor.

"Hang on," he told her as the garage door rumbled open.

He shifted into reverse and barreled out of the garage straight into the street, stopping only to shift back into Drive and take off down the road. The *dat-dat-dat* of gunfire rang in his ears and he heard several of the shots ping against the car. Ashlynn slid down in her seat to avoid the windows.

Garrett roared out of the neighborhood, employing all the skills he'd learned in driving during combat situations. Thankfully, traffic was light even when he hit the interstate, but he didn't let up until he'd determined for certain no one was following them. They'd escaped again, but it hadn't been clean. Stephen was dead and Jacob was still missing. But how had the killer tracked Ashlynn there? And why kill Stephen if they were after her? Was it possible this was all about something Stephen had been into? He needed to know more about Ashlynn's ex.

He turned to her to demand more information but stopped himself when he saw she was shaking. Her arms were folded over her chest and she appeared small and frightened in the lush leather seat.

Garrett came to a stop at the side of the road and pulled her close.

She wrapped her arms around him and pressed her face deep into his shoulder as sobs racked her body. She had every right to be upset. She'd been through a lot in the past several hours. Her son was missing, both her nanny and her ex-husband were dead, and someone was trying to kill her, too.

He might not be able to ever be a real part of her life, but Garrett knew he wouldn't rest until Jacob was back safely in her arms.

"What do we do now?" Ashlynn asked when her tears were spent.

She knew she should pull away from Garrett's embrace, but she couldn't. She felt safer here with him than she had since this mess started. If anyone could help her through this and get her son back alive, it was Garrett.

"I'll call Vince and let him know about Stephen, then we'll head to my house. You'll be safe there, I promise."

He drove while Ashlynn tried to keep her bubbling emotions in check. She hated that she'd lost control. He'd been understanding about it, but she didn't like being so vulnerable in front of Garrett. She had to keep her emotions in check around him or she would be of no help in finding her son. She needed to remain strong, at least until they found Jacob. After that, Garrett would be on his way, moving on with his life and she with hers.

He pulled into the driveway of a craftsman-style house in a neighborhood she recognized and led her inside. The house was neat and orderly but homey. Garrett motioned toward the living room. "I'll take the couch tonight. You can have the bedroom."

She nodded absently. Of all that had happened to her tonight, being here seemed the most surreal. She'd first met Garrett when she was placed in a group home after her foster mother had nearly killed her. He'd been young and rebellious, and into more trouble than she'd known at the time. She hadn't fallen for him then, but many years later, when they reconnected at a party given by one of her college friends, she'd fallen hard and fast.

He went to a cabinet and pulled something out of a box. It was a cell phone. "I know you lost yours this afternoon. This one is clean and no one can track you with it. I'm not planning on us splitting up, but in case it happens you'll be able to contact me." He quickly programmed his number into it then handed her the phone. "Do you have any other electronic devices on you that the killer could be using to locate you?"

She shook her head. "No, everything I had was in the car when it exploded. Why?"

"The killer found you at Stephen's house. Possibly he was there for Stephen, but we need to be sure he doesn't have some way of finding you." He reached out and took her hand, an act that put her nerve endings on alert. "Don't worry, Ashlynn. We'll figure out who is after you and why. And I promise you I won't rest until we've found your son and brought him home."

She thanked him again for his help, claimed she was tired and went upstairs. While it was true she was exhausted, she wouldn't be getting any sleep tonight. How could she with Jacob still missing?

She pulled out the phone Garrett had given her and dialed her friend and neighbor, Olivia Williams, thinking she should at least let someone know she was safe. But it was more than that. She longed for someone to talk to about what was happening.

Olivia sounded stunned to hear from her. "I thought you were dead," she whispered, her voice choked with grief. "Your house is surrounded by police and crowds. The news has been saying there was a shooting there and a woman was killed."

"It wasn't me," Ashlynn told her, then recounted the events of the night.

Once the shock of the situation wore off, Olivia

turned to worrying about Ashlynn's safety. "So where are you now? Are you safe?"

"I'm safe. Remember I told you about my old friend Garrett Lewis?"

"The hunky army ranger?"

She smiled at Olivia's very accurate description of him. "That's the one. I ran into him at the courthouse this afternoon. I'm with him. If anyone can help me find Jacob, it's him."

"I hope you're right. Jacob is such a sweet little boy. He doesn't deserve this. I'm just happy you're alive," Olivia said. "I thought I'd lost my best friend. Is there anything else I can do?"

"I don't know," Ashlynn said honestly. "The police will probably question you if they haven't already. If there's anything you can tell them that might help find Jacob…"

"Of course. I just don't know how helpful I can be. I didn't see anything. In fact, the first I'd heard about this was from the news." She huffed. "That just goes to prove you can't believe everything you see on television. Be safe. I'll be praying for you," Olivia told her before hanging up.

Ashlynn clicked off with her friend. She was glad she'd phoned her and glad Olivia was the praying type. Maybe God would listen to her and intervene to bring Jacob home safely. Ashlynn suspected they would need all the prayers they could get.

Garrett stretched out fully clothed on the couch. His mind was alert, replaying every moment of the night.

Someone with serious firepower was after Ashlynn, and there was no denying that. That man had come prepared to kill her. Garrett knew she was terrified. He'd been in combat, was trained and experienced to handle such incidents, but he'd certainly never expected to come across them in his hometown in Mississippi.

He liked Vince and the other guys he worked with, but he couldn't say he trusted any of them with his life. There were only five men who'd garnered that kind of confidence—Josh, Colton, Matt, Levi and Blake, all that remained of his ranger squad after the ambush. Since the night the rest of his friends, including his best friend, Marcus, were killed, trusting had come as hard for him as it had for the others. They'd been betrayed by someone they'd relied upon, their translator, who'd turned out to be an enemy spy.

He glanced at the ceiling, knowing that Ashlynn was only one floor away from him yet they remained so far apart. He'd chosen this life and he deserved it, but a pang of jealousy still nipped at him that she'd gotten on with her life. She'd married and started a family. Logic told him he had no right to be angry about that, but when had logic ever factored into his feelings?

He should have died on that mountain with his friends, but God had allowed him to live and there had to be a reason for that. He thought that reason might be sleeping upstairs in his bed right now. She needed him and, if he was honest, it felt good to have her need him again. He'd been crazy to let her go. It had taken him years to realize he'd made the biggest mistake of his life. He didn't deserve her and he knew she could never love him again after all that he'd done, but he couldn't deny he still cared for her.

A light shone through the living room window, grabbing his attention. It was a red light, like the kind on high-powered targeting rifles. He knew exactly what it was the moment he saw it. The killer had found them.

He slid from the couch to the floor and crawled toward the hall where he'd be able to safely stand without being exposed. He had to get to Ashlynn and warn her. They had only minutes to escape before the killer came bursting through the door, and Garrett had no way of knowing how many there were. He'd only seen one man at her house, but the more he considered it, the more he thought the shooter had made it inside a little too quickly. He might not have been acting alone.

But how had they been found, and so quickly? No one knew he and Ashlynn had a connection so no one should know to look for her here. Yet here they were, approaching with guns, ready to kill her as if stealing away her child wasn't punishment enough for whatever the reason was behind this attack.

Garrett burst through the bedroom door and Ashlynn jerked up from the bed. She was also fully clothed and lying on top of the covers. "We have to go," he said. "They found us." He stopped at his closet and pulled out his emergency gun bag. He kept it loaded with weapons and ammunition for situations just like this. His time with the rangers, as well as his freelance jobs, had taught him to always be ready to protect his back.

Leading her down the stairs and to the side door, he handed over the keys to the BMW while pulling a rifle from his go bag along with his night-vision goggles, which he slipped on. "You run to the car and start it up. I'm going to give us some cover fire." She nodded at his instructions.

He raised the weapon and stepped out, scanning the landscape for any trace of movement. He didn't want to just fire blindly. This was a family neighborhood, and he didn't want to take the risk of unintentional casualties. As Ashlynn reached the BMW, he saw movement behind a bush. He held his breath, waiting to make sure it wasn't a stray dog or a possum. Through his NVGs he saw the figure of a man rise and the outline of a weapon point at the vehicle. Garrett pulled the trigger, taking out the intruder as the engine on the BMW revved up. The man fell unmoving behind the bush where he'd been hiding. Garrett jumped into the car, aware that if the shooter was wearing a bulletproof vest, he would be back on his feet soon. Ashlynn quickly backed out of the driveway and took off down the street before more shooters became visible. But the sounds of gunfire from another direction as they roared away played in his ears confirming to him that whoever was after Ashlynn wasn't acting alone. He prayed none of his neighbors had been collateral damage.

Ashlynn attempted to concentrate on the road, but the thumping of her heart in her chest demanded all her attention. She tried to push through the trembling fear that raced into every nerve in her body, steadying her breath and gripping the steering wheel until her knuckles were pale. And she didn't let up on the accelerator, either. Thankfully, the roads were nearly deserted this time of night.

Over her pounding heart, she heard a noise and realized Garrett was speaking to her. She turned to look at him. His face was flushed with adrenaline, but that was the only sign that some madman had been shooting up his house mere minutes ago. "You can slow down now. We're not being followed."

She nodded, but her hands seemed glued to the steering wheel and her foot to the pedal. Finally, he touched her arm. "You want to pull over and let me drive?"

"No, I'm fine," she said. Her voice was clipped and edgy. She hadn't meant it to be. She was just trying to hold all her emotions together, but she wasn't stopping this car for anything, not now, not until her heart returned to a normal beat and she was certain no one was behind them.

"How did they find us?" she asked him.

"I don't know," he admitted. "I disabled the GPS on our phones and on the car. You said you didn't have anything on you that could be tracked. So they can't be tracking us electronically. It has to be someone who knows our whereabouts, but the only person I told was Vince. I suppose anyone who works around the police would know about our reconnection, but other than that, who is even aware we know one another?"

Her gut constricted at that suggestion. Had someone in the police department betrayed them to a killer?

He pulled out his phone. "I'm going to call my friend Josh Adams. He's a former ranger buddy who lives here in town. His wife works at the FBI office in Jackson. They're good people."

She glanced at him, nervousness ticking through her. "How do you know you can trust him?"

"There's no one I trust more than my fellow rangers. Josh is on our side. If I can't believe in anything else, I believe that."

"I can't trust him. I don't even know him."

He looked at her, eyes wide and surprised. He must have seen the fear on her—it had to be pouring off of her—because he gave her a reassuring nod and his voice quieted. "Then maybe you can trust me? I know I let you down before when I promised you'd be safe at my house. You weren't and that's on me. But believe me now, Ash. We absolutely can count on Josh." He held up his phone as if asking her permission to make the call.

She pondered the decision only for a moment. She had no choice, really. She needed to trust someone and it wasn't his fault she hadn't been safe at his house.

Finally, she nodded and he hit the button and placed the call.

She gripped the steering wheel again and took a deep breath, hoping against hope she could believe in Garrett's judgment about his friend.

He put the phone on speaker and when Josh answered, Garrett quickly updated him on the attacks against Ashlynn and the kidnapping.

"I heard about that on the news. How can I help?"

"We need a safe place to stay. Whoever is after Ashlynn is still managing to track us. I haven't figured out how yet. We need somewhere off the grid."

"I have just the place," Josh said. "Elise has a great-uncle who left her a cabin outside of town. No one should be able to trace it to you. I'm texting you the address of a convenience store. I'll meet you there in a half hour with the keys and a map to the cabin."

When he received the text, he called out the directions to Ashlynn and she headed north on the interstate. Rain turned to sleet as she drove and the quiet in the car grew deafening. The windshield wipers swished back and forth in a timed motion. That and the hum of the tires against the road were the only sounds. She felt tension pouring from Garrett as he rummaged through his bag and checked his weapons. Seeing him in combat mode was unnerving. When she'd known him before, he'd been rakish and charming, a dangerous combination in itself, but she'd not seen this side of him until today. He'd grown into a serious and brooding man with muscles for days and firsthand knowledge of guns and ammunition. Five years had changed him from a boy to a man…but was he now a man she could count on to bring Jacob home?

As she added Stephen's death to the killer's toll on her life, she realized the truth. If she wanted to live long enough to find her son and bring him home, she had no choice but to trust Garrett.

They pulled into the convenience store but didn't see Josh's car. It had been hours since this mess first started and neither of them had eaten anything. They both needed food in their stomachs and a few hours of sleep if they hoped to keep their wits about them. "Let's go inside and get some provisions," Garrett suggested.

Ashlynn agreed and shut off the engine then followed him inside, but he couldn't help but notice she looked like she was moving on autopilot. He lifted a silent plea skyward. They needed God's help to get through this and he could only hope that the Almighty would look past his shortcomings to see how deserving Ashlynn was of His help. He had no right to ask God for anything, not after the mess he'd made of his life, but Ashlynn didn't deserve the danger she'd found herself in.

As he carried two bags of groceries to the car, Josh pulled up. He jumped from his car and greeted them both.

"I'm sorry to hear about your son," Josh told Ashlynn. "But I have every confidence you're in good hands with Garrett. I also phoned Elise and updated her about the situation." He glanced at Ashlynn again. "Elise is FBI. She specializes in child abductions. Unfortunately, she's in Nashville at the moment working as part of a task force. But she did promise to contact the locals and examine the evidence they've collected."

"Thank you for your help," Ashlynn said. "And thank your wife, too."

Josh handed Garrett a hand-drawn map to the cabin and the keys. "I'm glad to see you bought some supplies. We haven't been up there in quite a while so the cupboards are pretty bare. What else can I do?"

Garrett didn't hesitate. "The men who attacked us

had automatic weapons and a sniper's aim. I might need some backup before this is over."

Josh nodded. "I'll call around and see who else is close. How are you set for weapons?"

"I was able to grab my gun bag. It's enough to last as long as we don't get into a major firefight."

"I've also got a storage locker with weapons and ammunition. I'll get some things ready."

"Is all that really necessary?" Ashlynn asked.

"Let's hope not, but if it is, we'll be ready." Garrett wasn't going to find himself outgunned again.

Josh shook his hand firmly. "Be safe, and remember I'm only a phone call away if you need me. I'll be on alert."

"We will. Thanks, Josh."

He climbed back into the car, waving as he drove off.

Josh's handwritten map led him straight to the cabin. As he'd stated, it was isolated and set back on a lake in the woods. It was a perfect place to hide out and he couldn't imagine how anyone could find them here.

He led Ashlynn inside and she looked around, glancing through the window as the sun rose over the lake. The cabin, while isolated, had modern amenities. Garrett headed over to the kitchen and placed the grocery bags on the counter. It helped to keep his hands busy unpacking the groceries. They would have to stock up if they planned to stay there long, but for now, this would do. He heated up a can of soup, poured it into two mugs and handed one to Ashlynn, who had curled up on the couch, a blanket wrapped around her and her legs tucked beneath her.

She shook her head, not wanting the soup, but Garrett insisted. "You need it. You have to stay strong for Jacob, remember?"

She relented and took it from him, though she didn't drink any of it. "I don't understand why this is happening," she said instead, her voice small and frail. "I don't know why God is doing this to me. What have I ever done that I would deserve any of this?"

She hadn't had an easy life, but he knew better than most that life wasn't always fair. If he could go back in time and change things, he would. He longed to change the past and his actions. But all he could do was be here for her now, comfort her as best he could and do everything in his power to bring her son home safely to her.

He was a believer. Had asked Jesus into his heart during his first year with the rangers, and he felt certain God was watching out for Jacob. Yet he also knew bad things happened in this world and God didn't often intervene in man's sinful behavior. Evil existed on Earth. He knew it firsthand. He'd witnessed it in action and asked himself many times the same questions she was now asking him. Why did God allow bad things to happen?

"I don't have all the answers for you, Ash. I can't fix what has happened, but I can be here for you and Jacob. I want to be here for you."

Her eyes were cold and hard as she looked at him. "I wish I could believe you," she told him in a flat voice. "But I can't forget how you left us. You abandoned me when I needed you most, Garrett. How can I trust you now? How can I know for certain that you won't leave again?"

"I won't leave. I'm not that same person, Ash."

She shook her head. "Neither am I. I've been through too much to be that trusting young girl I once was. I always thought you were the one person in this world I could count on. Then you left me. You left me when I needed you more than I'd ever needed anyone."

He didn't understand exactly what she was talking about, but she didn't understand what he'd gone through, either. "I thought I was protecting you. I didn't mean to hurt you."

"It doesn't matter what your intention was. It still hurt." She wiped away a tear that slipped through. "And the way you cut me off after you'd made your decision was cruel. You wouldn't even speak to me. I sent you letters. I emailed you. But you never responded. I didn't even have any way to know for sure that you received them."

"I got your letters, Ashlynn, and your emails. But you have to understand, I thought I was protecting you. I looked at our future and all I saw was your pain and heartache if I married you."

"You made that future of pain and heartache come true for me when you abandoned us, Garrett."

Her words stopped him. "What do you mean *us*?" Stephen's words came back to him in a wave. *I'm not Jacob's biological father.* Did that mean…?

She placed the cup of soup on the table and turned to him, her eyes blazing with anger and indignation.

"You claim you didn't want to leave me to raise a family alone, but that's exactly what you left me to do. You turned me into a single parent."

He felt his face flush at the realization of what she was saying. "Are you telling me Jacob…?" He stopped, his question hanging in the air.

Her expression changed to one of confusion. "You said you'd received my letters and emails."

"Yes, I received them, but I didn't read them. I couldn't. I thought you were trying to change my mind. I never read them."

He set down his cup and stood, his turn to feel overwhelmed. She acted as if he'd known all along, as if her letters and emails had come with the words *you're going to be a father* written in big, bold letters across the front and in the subject line. Maybe if they had, he would have opened them.

She stood and touched his arm, the graze of her fingers whisper soft. He looked at her and saw tears pooled in her eyes and the sudden realization hit him that she'd believed all this time he'd known and he'd rejected her because of it.

Her manner softened but the truth hung out there for several moments that seemed to last an eternity. Finally, she spoke the words that would change his life forever.

"Garrett, Jacob is your son."

FOUR

Garrett lowered himself slowly back into the cushions of the couch. Hearing her words was a blow like no other he'd ever sustained. He was sick and excited at the same time. It was the strangest mixture of emotions he'd ever felt.

She sat beside him and placed her hand over his, her touch only serving to rev up the emotional turmoil he was currently experiencing. "I'm sorry. I thought you knew."

He raked a hand over his face as the weight of her words continued to sink in. "Are you telling me that I'm searching for my own son?"

"Yes."

He stood, his mind spinning with this new information. *His* son was the boy missing. His *son* was out there somewhere. Someone had kidnapped *his son*.

He spun around and glared at Ashlynn. "How could you let this happen?"

Hurt and anger flashed in her eyes, but she stood to face him, her chin jutting out stubbornly. "I don't even know why this is happening."

"You should have done a better job of protecting him."

Now her face flushed with anger. "Don't you dare stand there and criticize my parenting, Garrett Lewis. You were the one who ran out on us."

"Not by choice."

"Do you think that matters? Do you believe for one second that your intentions make any difference in our lives? You promised you would help me find Jacob and bring him home. Once that's done, you can leave again and never have to worry about us."

She turned and rushed into the bedroom, slamming the door behind her. He heard the click of the lock and grimaced at his own reaction. What was he doing? He was taking out his frustrations on her and that wasn't fair. She already had too many people blaming her for her choices. He didn't want to be one of them.

He stood at the back door and stared out at the lake, his mind struggling to process this new information that changed everything he knew about his life. Every decision would now have to be made in the context of how it would affect his child. The idea terrified him. He'd never had a dad and he had no idea how to be one. His best friend, Marcus, who had died in the ambush, had always had his family in his thoughts, or so it seemed, because he always had a funny story to share about something that had happened when he was home or else he was showing off a drawing one of his kids had colored for him.

In Garrett's mind, that was what a father looked like. *His* first official act as a father had been to abandon the mother of his child. Now he'd accused her of allowing his abduction. Not a great start to fatherhood.

He pushed the door open and walked outside, needing the brisk morning air to clear his mind. He stared up at the sky and had to question why God would allow this to happen. Why had he been allowed to live while a terrific dad like Marcus had been taken? He tried to shake those feelings away. He couldn't let emotion and guilt jeopardize what he needed to do. He had to focus on the job of finding Jacob. Everything else could be worked out once he was home safe and sound.

Yet even as that thought crossed his mind, another countered it. If he'd been killed instead of Marcus, who would be here to look for his son now? Jacob's safety would be in the hands of strangers. He liked several of the men he'd met on the force, but did he trust any one of them to find his kid? The answer was a resounding *no*.

He picked up a stick and hurled it into the lake.

For the first time since the night of the ambush, he couldn't feel guilty for staying alive because it allowed him to be here now when his son needed him.

Ashlynn flung herself across the bed, angry at him for letting her down again and even more at herself for daring to believe in him. He couldn't have faked that reaction. He honestly hadn't known she was pregnant when he'd broken their engagement. But that gave him no right to blame her for Jacob being kidnapped.

But her anger extended even further. Life had once again used her as a pawn in its game and Ashlynn wasn't amused. She didn't understand why God continued to allow such terrible events to happen to her. She'd never done anything to the Great Almighty.

Tears slipped from her eyes as she remembered her foster mother telling her she'd offended God just by being born. She'd had no control over that or over any of the terrible events that had made up her life. Her mother's death along with her father's alcoholism had led her into foster care and into the home of Kathryn Rollins, who had singled her out for a reason only she knew to suffer repeated abuse and neglect. The other children in the home—six in all, including Kathryn's own biological son—had not shared in her torment, and Ashlynn had grown up believing something was inherently wrong with her.

She often still pondered that thought. Did she truly not deserve a family of her own? Or a happy life for her son? Judge Warren would call that kind of thinking utter nonsense and assure her that she did, indeed, deserve such things. But the older she got and the more she struggled, the less she tended to believe it.

But that didn't mean she would quit fighting, if not for herself then for Jacob's sake. He deserved a happy life even if she didn't.

A few hours later, Garrett heated up two breakfast burritos he'd gotten at the convenience store. It wasn't much, but it was all he had to offer until they made a run for supplies. He tensed when he heard the bedroom door unlock. He watched Ashlynn walk out and shuffle across the floor to the kitchen. She looked better after a few hours of rest, but he doubted she'd slept well. He also couldn't miss the red, swollen eyes that indicated she'd spent at least part of the time crying. He kicked himself, feeling guilty for causing at least some of that.

"I made breakfast," he said, sliding a burrito to her. She hadn't eaten any of the soup he'd heated for her earlier, which meant she hadn't eaten since before he'd first seen her yesterday afternoon.

She shook her head at the offer of food. "Just coffee, please."

He poured her a cup from the pot he'd started and handed it to her. Then he sighed and got ready to eat crow. "Look, Ash, I owe you an apology. I think I was taking out my frustrations on you earlier. I was just so shocked by what you told me."

She sipped her coffee, but her expression was guarded as she glanced at him. "No apology is required."

He saw the lift of her chin and the determined look in her eye. He knew that stance. She was shutting herself down, hiding her hurt and pain away so she wouldn't seem weak. He'd seen her do it before. If she could protect herself, then she would never have to admit to being hurt.

"Don't do that. Don't shut me out like that."

"I don't know what you're talking about. I'm fine."

He walked around the island separating them. "I'm trying to say I'm sorry I hurt you, and before you say I didn't, I know good and well I did. I was wrong to blame you for Jacob's abduction. You had no control over what some psychotic did." He reached out and caressed her arm. He'd wanted to comfort her but instead he'd jabbed her. He longed now to pull her into his arms. She looked like a wounded bird, so sad and helpless, but he knew from experience that that look was deceiving. She was a mother lion who would pounce when her cub was in danger.

"You only said what everyone is probably thinking. This is my fault."

"Anyone who knows you understands how much that little boy means to you."

He did pull her into his arms now, drawing her closer and pressing her against him. After a moment, she burrowed her head into his chest and he was glad he could at least offer her a shoulder on which to cry. But he didn't expect the dizzying way the scent of her shampoo or the feel of her soft, smooth skin made him feel.

"I just want him back," she whispered and the torment in her voice made his heart constrict. She stared up into his eyes, but something about her expression told him she wasn't seeing him right at that moment. She reached up and touched his face. "Jacob has your eyes." Tears pooled in hers.

He caressed her cheek and found her leaning into his hand. His eyes fell on her lips and he remembered the sweet taste of them that had never strayed far from his memory. How many nights had he dreamed about holding her again? Now she was here, in his arms, needing his comfort. Her chin lifted again and this time it wasn't out of defiance. Her lips were close to his and he breathed in the heady scent of her. Even after a day of car bombs and running for her life, she smelled sweet, like cucumber. He wanted so much to kiss her, to rekindle the spark that had once been between them.

But he didn't.

He pulled himself away emotionally and then physically before he crossed a line and enveloped her lips with his. He shouldn't get to go on with his life when others didn't. Marcus would never kiss his wife again. Why shouldn't Garrett face similar consequences?

His phone rang and he gave a deep, relieved sigh. Seeing it was Vince, he put some distance between Ashlynn and himself as he pressed the answer key and placed the call on speaker.

"Hey, Vince. Any news?"

"Some. We've scheduled a press conference for eleven a.m. It's time we address the public. I'd like Ashlynn to say a few words if she's up to it."

Ashlynn nodded. "Of course I will."

"Good. I'll see you both at the precinct."

Garrett pressed the button to end the call. Narrowing his eyes, he gave Ashlynn a quizzical look. "Are you sure you're up for a press conference?"

But she batted away tears and straightened her shoulders in steady determination. "It won't be easy, but I'll do whatever I need to do to bring home Jacob."

"Well, you won't have to do it alone." He placed a reassuring hand on her shoulder. It wasn't much after how close he'd come to kissing her, but it was the best he could offer. "I'll be right there beside you."

* * *

What had almost happened back there?

Ashlynn shook her head as she followed Garrett out to the car. She'd taken the time to shower and change, but she still couldn't push past that scene in the kitchen. He'd almost kissed her. She was certain he'd wanted to. But the real surprise had been her reaction. She hadn't pushed him away. She hadn't even told him no. In fact, she was quite certain that she'd encouraged him. Her face warmed at the idea that she'd practically thrown herself at him…and he'd rejected her. Again. Would she never learn her lesson? They were together in this only because they shared a son. No need to relive a relationship that had left her devastated. No, she wouldn't go down that path again. Her heart couldn't stand it.

They were both quiet as Garrett drove, and she was thankful for that. Other people might have believed they had to keep her talking and upbeat, but Garrett seemed to respect that she needed quiet to regroup. She'd never been one for chitchat and she didn't find comfort in having groups of people around her. She much preferred solitude and was glad Garrett remembered to give her that space.

He took the exit from the interstate into downtown Jackson then parked in the garage attached to the police station. He walked beside her, his hand reassuringly on her back as they entered the building.

Vince looked weary as he led them into the room they'd designated as a command center for her case. There was a large whiteboard up front where they posted photos and evidence relevant to the case. She saw her own photo along with the one of Jacob they'd used for the Amber Alert.

"Have there been any hits on the Amber Alert since we left last night?" she asked Vince.

Vince nodded. "We're continuing to follow up on them all but so far nothing solid. We were able to obtain video footage from several of your neighbors' security cameras that showed a suspicious white van in the area. We ran the tag and discovered it was stolen from a dry cleaner's two days ago. Someone removed the decals but it's the same van. We added that description to the Amber Alert and several people have reported seeing it, but unfortunately that type of van is very popular with businesses."

She stared at the crime scene photos of Stephen and Mira. Their deaths seemed so brutal and so unnecessary. But, then again, was murder ever necessary? Ashlynn knew they were dealing with someone with no respect for human life, and that frightened her because this was also the person who had her son. She closed her eyes as a wave of sorrow washed over her. Had Jacob witnessed Mira's death? How scared he would have been. A motherly ache pulsed through her and her arms yearned to hold him and reassure him that everything was going to be fine.

Garrett's hand touched her back again and she found it comforting to have him so close. It was just the strength she needed to push through her maternal emotions and look at this case with a prosecutor's eye.

"Has forensics found anything from the crime scenes that might be helpful?"

Vince obviously noticed her change and he perked up, too, and went into total business mode. "According to the medical examiner's preliminary notes, the attacker slashed Mira's throat from behind. Based on the angle of the incision, he would have to be right-handed and at least six feet tall. He also found material beneath her nails, so it looks like Mira scratched the perpetrator during the struggle. He's running it for DNA. Hopefully, we'll get a hit but that will take a while. We're still waiting on fingerprints and fibers found at the scene.

"Also, we've been looking into Mira's background, but so far we haven't identified any risks in her life that could have made her a target. We haven't found any prior drug use or connections to criminal elements. According to family and friends we've interviewed, she didn't have any romantic attachments and no one knew of anyone who might want her dead. As of right now, unless we receive any new information, we're going to operate under the assumption that her death was collateral damage in the attack on you and your family. I've got detectives following up on recently released prisoners with either a connection to you or a history of crimes against children."

She nodded, thinking the police were doing all they could to put a good case together for prosecution. But it didn't help get them any closer to finding her son. She stared at the board. Mira's leads had fallen through and the Amber Alert tips hadn't yet produced any viable leads.

"What about the bomb in my car?"

Vince grimaced. "So far, not much. No witnesses saw anyone suspicious around your car yesterday. However the fire marshal does believe military-type explosives were used to detonate the bomb. It wasn't the make-it-in-your-basement type."

"So we're dealing with someone who has access to automatic weapons and explosives," Garrett stated wryly. "Terrific."

"What can I do?" Ashlynn asked Vince. "I need to do something."

"Going through your case files is the best thing you can do right now. You know those cases better than anyone else. You'll be more likely to notice something that stands out. And hopefully this press conference will elicit some other leads for us to follow up on."

She felt her insides begin to quiver. Jacob was out there somewhere, possibly hurt and definitely frightened, and they were no closer to bringing him home than they had been the moment he'd been taken. She folded her arms across her chest to try to maintain her composure and scanned the room. These men were doing all they could to find Jacob, but even she knew their abilities were limited. They could follow leads but once those leads went cold, the chances of finding Jacob diminished. She knew the statistics. Kids who weren't recovered in the first forty-eight hours were unlikely to be found alive...and time was ticking down for finding Jacob. But without God on her side, she wasn't sure that was going to happen.

* * *

Ashlynn braced herself as she and Garrett crossed the street and entered the building that housed the offices of the district attorney. Her coworkers, with their pitying glances and sorrowful expressions, were the worst. She didn't want to be here where all this emotion might make her totter over the edge, but she needed to do something to occupy her mind or else she wouldn't have to worry about other people's sympathies pushing her over the edge of reason. She would slide there all on her own.

Again, Garrett's hand on her back was a comforting support. Her gratitude at having him beside her outweighed her desire to flee from him and wallow in her anger and bitterness at how he'd rejected her again this morning. Each time the thought popped into her head, she pushed it back, reminding herself that she'd been emotional and she had a history of making bad choices out of emotion instead of reason. She couldn't be that person any longer. Jacob was depending on her to be logical. She needed Garrett to bring Jacob home and that angered her. She shouldn't need his help. He didn't deserve to be able to abandon them and then swoop in and be needed. It wasn't right. But then nothing about this situation was fair.

She headed for her office and Garrett closed the door behind them. Walking to her desk, she slid into her chair, basking in the familiar comfort of it. Being a prosecutor had been her dream for a long time, ever since she'd found herself testifying against her foster mother and becoming friends with Judge Warren. Then only an ADA, he had walked her through the process, then taken her under his wing, mentoring her throughout college and law school. He admired her tenacity and determination, he'd told her. He'd been a wonderful support for her and she wasn't sure she would have made it to the position she was in without him. Now this was her office and she was good at her job. But she would gladly give it all up to have her son back.

Garrett's phone buzzed at his side. He glanced at the screen. "They need me across the street. I'd rather you not leave the office. I'll come get you when they're ready for the press conference."

She nodded. "I always keep a spare makeup bag in my desk. I'll try to look my best."

Bridgette Myers, her assistant, rushed into the office. She stared after Garrett as he left, her eyes wide and her mouth open in surprise, and Ashlynn saw her mouth the word *wow* as she approached Ashlynn and enveloped her in a hug.

"How are you holding up?" Bridgette asked. "I cannot believe this is happening to you. A car bomb? Being shot at? Your son kidnapped and your ex-husband murdered?" She listed the previous day's events as if Ashlynn hadn't lived through them. "I just cannot believe someone I know has this happening to her." She handed over a cup of coffee and Ashlynn thanked her once she stopped talking long enough to take a breath.

"I won't be here long," Ashlynn said. "I'm going to be part of a press conference about Jacob's abduction—"

"I heard about that," Bridgette interrupted. "I can't believe it's come to that."

"I just stopped by for my extra jacket and makeup bag that I keep in my desk."

"Sure, the one you use before court."

"That's right. The police also want me to look through my case files for the last several months. Could you gather those together and have them ready for me to take with me after the press conference?"

"Sure. No problem. Can I do anything else for you, Ashlynn?"

"No, not really, although I don't believe I'll be very productive on my current cases. I wonder if I can get Roger to reassign them until Jacob is found." Roger was the ADA in charge of case assignments.

"I don't see why he wouldn't. I've heard people talking already this morning and everyone is willing to help out however they can. I'll take care of it."

Her door swung open and Ken stepped inside. "Ashlynn!" He pulled her into a hug and he was like a big papa bear. She and Ken had become close over the past six months since he'd joined their staff. Although he worked for the entire office, Ashlynn noticed he volunteered to take on a lot of her cases.

"I know you have other cases to work on," she told Ken, "so I appreciate you taking the time to help with finding Jacob."

He waved away her thanks. "Whatever I can do to help, I will. I want to be involved with this, Ashlynn. He's a cute little fella and I don't want to see anything happen to him. Whatever you need, I want you to call me."

She nodded. "I will." She glanced from Ken to

Bridgette and felt a rush of tears burn her eyes. It meant so much to her to have friends like these during this difficult time. "I want to thank both of you for being here for me. It means a lot." She gulped back emotion. She didn't have many friends, and that was by choice. She'd learned at a young age that letting people into your life generally meant letting them hurt you, and that instinct to keep people at arm's length had only been confirmed by Garrett's desertion. But these were two people she worked closely with and she considered them both much more than mere coworkers. Bridgette's eagerness to help in any way and Ken's experience-filled encouragement had garnered her trust in them both.

Bridgette's eyes filled with tears and she dabbed them away. "I'll go start gathering those files for you," she said, then hurried out.

"Files?" Ken asked. "What files?"

"My case files. Garrett and Vince are convinced Jacob's abduction might have something to do with one of my cases, so I said I would go through them and see if anything stood out."

"Ashlynn, I'm taking care of that. I've already started searching through them. I haven't come across anything suspicious so far, but I'm making progress."

"I know, but a second pair of eyes never hurt. Besides, I need something to do besides sitting around making myself crazy wondering if Jacob is safe."

He nodded as if that notion hadn't occurred to him. "Of course. I'll help Bridgette gather those files and bring them over to the police station so you'll have them after the press conference."

She thanked him and watched him walk out. She went back to her desk and pulled out her makeup bag, knowing she would need a ton of concealer to hide the bags under her eyes this morning. She pushed it away. It didn't matter what she looked like. Today, she wasn't a professional prosecutor. She was just a mother whose child had been snatched from her. No one would care how she looked.

She picked up a stack of mail on her desk and sorted through it, instead. She tore one envelope open and pulled out a sheet of paper. A photo fell to the desk. She picked it up and saw it was a snapshot of Mira with Jacob at the playground. She turned it over and her heart stopped as she read the scrawled words across the back.

What kind of mother leaves raising her child to someone else? You don't deserve to be a mother.

Ken walked Ashlynn across the street to the police station. Garrett met them at the door and once she was safely inside, he loaded the box of files Ken carried into his truck. The police had retrieved it from Stephen's house during their investigation into his murder, and he'd been glad to trade in the BMW for his own vehicle. "Thank you for doing this for Ashlynn," Garrett said.

"Absolutely," Ken said. "I never had kids of my own so I consider Ashlynn to be like a daughter—or maybe a kid sister since we're not that far apart in age. That little lady holds a special place in my heart even though I've only known her a few months." He glanced at Garrett. "Do you have any kids?"

Garrett's heart skipped a beat. If Ken had asked him that question yesterday, the answer would have been different. But he was in no mood to explain all that to anyone. Ashlynn could share that story if she chose to. His mind was still trying to wrap itself around the fact that he was a dad. It still seemed unreal.

"I'm glad she's got someone else watching her back," Garrett told him instead then shook the man's hand.

"Take care of her," Ken said, then he marched across the street to the DA's offices.

Garrett headed back into the police station. He poured two cups of coffee and handed Ashlynn one of them. Her hands were shaking, and he knew it wasn't because she was chilly. She tightened her fingers around the cup and breathed in the coffee vapor.

Dressed in smart slacks and a blouse, she looked beautiful but sad. She was wearing that expression he knew so well, the one that was full of utter despair and hopelessness. He'd seen it before and he hated it even more now. She couldn't lose hope. He would find her son…his son…their son. He sighed. His brain was still trying to comprehend what he'd learned last night and he was more determined than ever to find Jacob and bring him home. He'd made a promise to Ashlynn and he meant to keep it.

The press conference was a good idea, although he still wasn't sure Ashlynn was up for it. But she had to be, and he wasn't leaving her side until it was over. He sat beside her and tried to find words that would reassure her. "We'll find him, Ashlynn. We'll bring him home."

Her chin quivered and tears pooled in her eyes. "This is my fault."

He sighed wearily. They'd already been through this. "No, it absolutely is not. I had no right to suggest it was. I was wrong and I'm sorry."

"I wish everyone believed that." She reached into her pocket and pulled out a slip of paper.

He opened it and saw the words scribbled on it. "Where did you get this?"

"It was on my desk with my mail."

He fought he urge to crumple the paper. It was evidence and he had to preserve it, but it was truly nothing but garbage. "No one believes this."

"Someone does."

"Ashlynn, you and I have both seen our share of terrible mothers. You are not like her. You would never intentionally hurt your child."

She shuddered. Few people besides Ashlynn would know he was referring to Kathryn Rollins, the foster mother who had nearly killed her. After suffering her abuse for years, Ashlynn had stood up to her and nearly been beaten to death for it. Had she again stood up to the wrong person and now her son was paying the price? He saw guilt written across her face and grabbed her arm turning her to him. "This is not your fault," he told her again, his tone pressing her to listen and believe him. "Jacob's abduction is not your fault. Someone is targeting you and I will find out who."

She stared up at him, her countenance full of hopelessness and despair. He was more determined than ever to wipe that expression from her face for good. But he knew he would need all of God's help to do so.

Please help me find Jacob and bring him home safely.

He couldn't concern himself with the logistics of what home meant yet. First he would find his son, then they would unravel everything else.

In preparation for the press conference, Ashlynn went to the ladies room and splashed her face with cold water. She was glad now that she hadn't bothered with the makeup because it would have just been washed away. She pulled on the jacket from her office, smoothed down her hair and stared at herself in the mirror in the ladies room.

Someone knocked on the door then opened it. Garrett stood protectively just outside. "They're ready for you, Ash."

She closed her eyes and tried to gather her confidence. She didn't know how she was going to get through this without breaking down. Vince had told her she didn't have to speak, but she knew she did.

Although she was still miffed at him for his words last night, she was glad Garrett was with her. His strength was a comfort to her in this trying time. She didn't know why God was allowing this to happen. Why Stephen had to die. Why Jacob had been kidnapped. She'd only thought her world was falling apart before when her marriage had ended, but now she knew she'd been so wrong.

The press was already set up outside the police station. And even though it was December, the day was mild and the bright lights were hot. As Vince stood to address the press, Ashlynn noticed he was sweating.

She listened to his official statement. "Yesterday evening, the body of twenty-one-year-old Mira Randolph was found murdered. Miss Randolph was working as a nanny for the family of Assistant District Attorney Ashlynn Morris. The child in her care, four-year-old Jacob Morris, was reported missing and is considered an endangered child. An Amber Alert has been issued. ADA Morris has been the target of multiple attempts on her life and the child's father was found murdered in his home late last night. We are coordinating with other law enforcement agencies in the state and surrounding states, as well as the FBI. Anyone with any information about these murders or the whereabouts of four-year-old Jacob Morris are instructed to phone the JPD. A tip line has been set up for any information the public has. All tips will be investigated."

Ashlynn didn't know how she was even still standing. The press was a blur surrounding her. Her only strength was Garrett behind her. She felt his presence holding her solid as Vince took questions from the reporters.

"Do you believe this has anything to do with ADA Morris's job as a prosecutor?" one of the reporters called out.

"We're investigating that possibility along with others."

After several more questions, which basically led to Vince's reassurance that they were investigating every possibility, he turned to Ashlynn. "ADA Morris has prepared a written statement. She will not be taking questions."

Vince moved aside and Ashlynn stepped to the podium. This wasn't the first time she had addressed the press. She knew most of their names. She'd met them before and discussed other cases. But this was different. Now, she had to face them not as a member of law enforcement, but as the victim of a crime. She didn't much like being on this side of the story.

She stared past the reporters and looked into the cameras, addressing the kidnapper. She took a deep breath to steady her nerves. She wanted to scream and rant and demand that Jacob be returned and even thought about threatening the kidnapper with full prosecution and every legal means she possessed, but she didn't. It was a given that the person responsible would be prosecuted, but she knew threats and rants would do no good right now. Whoever had taken Jacob from her wanted to see her emotionally fall apart. Was the kidnapper out there now, watching and waiting to see her lose it? She thought he was and decided he wouldn't get the satisfaction of seeing how his actions had affected her.

She held up the photograph that had been distributed to the press and spoke as calmly as she could. "My son, Jacob, is four years old. He's funny and he's smart and he loves playing with his blocks and watching cartoons. I know he's frightened and doesn't understand what is happening right now. He's only a little boy and I ask the person or persons who took him to please drop him off safely at a hospital or fire station. Whatever your problem with me, he is not a part of it. I don't know why you are targeting my family, but I'm begging you to please return Jacob. He misses his family and we miss him."

She stepped down as reporters shouted questions to her and snapped her picture. Vince returned and reminded them that Ashlynn would not be answering questions. She stepped off the podium and hurried into the safety of the courthouse before she broke down in front of the cameras. She wouldn't let them see her lose control, but she also knew she couldn't hold it back much longer.

She leaned against a wall, stopping to catch her breath and compose herself. It wasn't fair this was happening to her. Her little boy didn't deserve this. A wave of fury rushed through her and all the anger and bitterness she'd felt moments ago for the kidnappers now focused on God. He was the one who had allowed this to happen to them. He was the one who could have prevented it. Tears streamed down her face and she pounded her hands against the concrete walls.

As her emotion was spent, she realized she wasn't alone. She felt someone behind her watching her. She turned to see Garrett standing there, his face set and determined.

Suddenly, he grabbed her hand. "Come with me," he said, pulling her down the hall. "I have an idea I want to check out."

"What? Where are we going?" she demanded, wiping at her wet face.

He stopped and turned to her. "I may know a way to find your son."

FIVE

The idea had occurred to him during the press conference when he'd glanced at all the news vans parked near the courthouse steps. The white van the neighbors had seen might be the key to finding Jacob and he knew a way to possibly locate that van.

"Do you remember a guy named Mike Webb?"

"How can I forget him? I see his name on my roster every few months, but he always manages to avoid conviction."

He nodded. That was the guy. "He's a major player in the car theft business. At least, he used to be. I'm glad to know that hasn't changed."

They'd each shared their tales of difficult childhoods and bad choices they'd both made, so Garrett knew Ashlynn was aware he used to steal cars for Webb back in his younger days before the army cleaned him up.

"Well, I thought I might be able to track him down. Maybe he can tell us who might be into stealing white vans in town."

"They probably all wind up in his chop shop," she

said. "The police have put together a task force to track down the car-theft ring operating in town. They haven't been able to locate him. Why do you think you can?"

"Because he knows me. I used to work for him. He wasn't a bad guy. And I'm sure he would never be party to ripping a child from his mother."

"Garrett, he's a criminal."

"So was I," he reminded her. "Everyone deserves a second chance to do the right thing, don't they, Ash?"

She hesitated, perhaps wondering if he was talking about the car thieves or himself. Did she think he was hinting around that he wanted a second chance with her and Jacob? He hadn't really meant it that way and didn't want her to get the wrong impression.

He pressed the point. "You're searching through your recent convictions, you've got Ken looking into any recent prisoners released, and Vince and the police are following Amber Alert leads and investigating the deaths of your nanny and Stephen. I don't know if this will amount to anything, but if it might, shouldn't we follow it? I have to try."

"You didn't mention this to Vince?"

"No, because I don't know if it's going to go anywhere. I'd rather not get the police involved if it's just a dead end."

He wondered briefly if her duty as a prosecutor would hamper her ability to get on board with his idea. He didn't have to wait long to find out.

She nodded. "It's a good idea if you think he'll talk to you."

"I believe he will, only…" This was the part of the plan she wasn't going to like. "I don't think you should come with me. These guys may not want to talk if they know you're a prosecutor."

"Garrett, you were standing next to me during the press conference. Won't they have seen you on TV?"

"If anyone questions me about it, I'll just say you've hired me to find your son."

He knew she would prefer to go in with a full police task force and so would he, but they didn't even know yet where to search. Plus, this was a connection the police were unlikely to be able to provide.

He reached out and stroked her arm. "I don't want to leave you behind. I would prefer to have you with me. But in this case, I think it's necessary."

"No, I understand. You can't exactly get your former friends to open up to you with a prosecutor standing by your side. I'll stay at my office and use the time to look through my case files."

He nodded. "You should be safe there. No one is going to attack you in an office full of people."

He escorted her back to her office before he left.

He hadn't been lying when he'd said he would feel better having her with him, but her status as a prosecutor would only hinder him. He was better off working this lead alone.

Garrett chuckled, realizing there was a time not too long ago when working on his own would have been his preference, but not now. Not since Ashlynn had stepped back into his life.

Ashlynn had a difficult time concentrating on her case files. The words and information seemed to merge together. She couldn't focus because all she could think about was Jacob and wondering if he was safe, and Garrett and wondering if he was making any progress. It seemed the police weren't getting any closer to finding Jacob. She hoped Garrett was having more success.

A knock on her door made her look up. She smiled, happy to see Judge Warren step inside. "Come in," she exclaimed, welcoming him into the office. She reached up and hugged his neck. He was one of the few people who'd been there for her throughout the years and she cherished his friendship and advice.

"I saw the press conference. I'm sorry this is happening to you. Do the police have any leads about your son?"

"They're following several, but nothing concrete so far."

"I'm so sorry to hear that." He handed her a plate with plastic wrap on it. "My wife made these brownies. I remember how you used to like them so I thought I would bring them by. It's not much, but it's the least I can do."

She smiled at the gesture. She'd been a twelve-year-old battered girl the first time he'd offered her some of his wife's brownies and, yes, she had liked them. He'd never forgotten that, and every now and then he brought her some. And it was always too many. Generally, she took a couple for her and Jacob then placed the rest in the break room for the office to share. But his gesture meant the world to her because it proved that someone did care about her. She took the plate and gave him a big hug and a sincere thank-you.

"If I can do anything to help, please call."

"I will, Judge. Thank you."

He turned and sauntered out, and Ashlynn spotted Bridgette standing by her door. She walked in holding a steaming cup of coffee.

"Oh, brownies," she exclaimed, used to indulging in the treats from Judge Warren's wife.

Ashlynn laughed at the familiarity of the situation. It made her feel just a bit better. "Help yourself," she told Bridgette.

Bridgette set down the coffee, unwrapped the plastic and bit into one of the brownies. A satisfied look crossed her face. "So good," she said. "Mrs. Warren sure knows her stuff when it comes to baking."

"She always has." Ashlynn took a few of the brownies from the plate then replaced the cover and handed it to Bridgette. "Would you place these in the break room for everyone to share?"

"Sure. Oh, I brought this for you." She pushed the coffee toward Ashlynn. "I thought you could use it."

"Thank you. I could." She bit into one of the brownies and washed it down with the coffee.

"How's it coming?" Bridgette asked. "Are you finding anything?"

"Not yet, but I won't give up. If there's something in these files that can help tell me who took my son, I will find it."

"I'll let you get back to work, then." Bridgette walked out, carrying the plate of brownies with her while Ashlynn turned back to the files.

She meant what she'd said about not giving up. Judge Warren had always encouraged her to fight for what she wanted and this was one fight she wouldn't lose. She would find a way to bring Jacob home.

But she realized she wasn't fighting alone and that gave her comfort. Garrett was out there now, tracking down leads. She was thankful he'd come back into her life just when she needed him and his skills as a ranger. She thought about her earlier railing at God. She didn't know if Garrett's return to town was divine intervention or just plain good timing, but she was thankful nonetheless.

She spent the next half hour poring over her records but then her eyes began to blur. She was having trouble concentrating and realized she'd read the same passage three times and still didn't know what it said.

She rubbed the bridge of her nose. Her eyes were tired and she supposed the strain was finally catching up with her. She glanced at her coffee cup, now empty again. She needed a refill, but instead of bothering Bridgette she got up to fetch it herself. She needed to walk, to stretch her legs and get her blood pumping or else she was going to fall asleep at her desk. She forced her legs to move. They felt like dead weight as she left her office and headed down the hall. Maybe she should have buzzed Bridgette instead, she thought, but it was too late for that.

She entered the break room and saw no one was there. That was a relief because she wasn't up to making awkward chitchat with her coworkers or rehashing all that had happened. There was a full pot of coffee, though, and it was still warm so someone had made it recently. For that, she was thankful.

She poured some into her mug and doctored it the way she liked. Her brain still seemed to be in a fog and she felt groggy. And the coffee didn't seem to help. She gripped the counter as the room began to spin. Something was wrong. She shouldn't be this tired. She felt more like…more like she'd been drugged. She saw the plate of brownies on the table. That was the only thing she'd eaten recently. But it couldn't be…they couldn't be. She stumbled to a chair and fell into it.

Suddenly, someone grabbed her from behind. Something tight and hard dug into her neck. She was being choked!

She pulled at her neck, trying to dislodge whatever was cutting off her air supply, then flailed her arms behind her. They felt like stone pillars and moving them was difficult, but she kicked and clawed and fought, knowing she had to do whatever she could to survive.

Her attacker pulled her to her feet and Ashlynn's head started spinning. She fought the urge to lose consciousness, knowing it would be the end of her. Fear pulsed through her and she wished Garrett was there. She reached up and jabbed at her attacker's face, hoping to connect with his eyes. Her fingernails dug into something like fabric. A mask. Just like the man who'd been shooting at her at her house had been wearing.

One of her kicks hit the cabinet and sent her coffee mug falling. It hit the floor, shattered and coffee splattered. It was hot when it hit her and Ashlynn groaned but her attacker did, too, obviously splashed with the scalding liquid. He loosened his grip just enough that

Ashlynn managed to get her hands between her neck and the offending wire he was using to choke her.

She heard footsteps and voices, and her attacker swore and shoved her. Her head hit the cabinet hard as she went down to the floor. When she looked back up, the break room door was swinging shut and he was gone.

She glanced at her hand, which was cut and bleeding either by a shard from her coffee mug or the wire her attacker had choked her with. Her fingernails had also snagged pieces of the mask he'd used to cover his face.

The door opened and Ashlynn tensed. Had he returned to finish her off? Bridgette stepped inside and Ashlynn breathed a sigh of relief. Hers must have been the footsteps that had frightened her attacker off.

"Ashlynn!" Bridgette rushed to her side, crunching on the shards and kneeling beside her. "Are you okay? What happened?" She hurried back to the door and opened it, shouting out. "Someone get help. Ashlynn's been attacked."

Pain was radiating from her neck, but the dull throb from her head overshadowed it. She'd hit the cabinet hard and the room was spinning, but that could also have been from being drugged.

"You're bleeding," Bridgette said grabbing for a towel and pressing it to Ashlynn's forehead, where she hadn't even known she'd been hit. She must have fallen on one of the shards or cut herself when she hit the cabinet.

"Who did this to you?" Bridgette asked, her face full of concern.

A wave of nausea rolled over Ashlynn before she could respond. She leaned over and the next thing she knew she was flat on her back. Bridgette's worried face hovered over hers then faded away as Ashlynn slipped into darkness.

Garrett hurried to the ER when he got the call from Vince about Ashlynn being attacked at her office. He kicked himself for being so foolish. He never should have left her, but at the time it had seemed like the only way. He'd never dreamed she would be in danger in her own office.

He hurried inside and found the room where she was being observed. His gut clenched when he saw her lying on the bed. She looked small beneath the hospital blanket and had an IV hooked up to her and a bandage across her forehead and around her hand. But she managed to give him a weak smile when she saw him. "Hi."

He reached for her non-bandaged hand and squeezed it, as much to comfort himself as to comfort her. "What happened?"

"Someone attacked me in the break room. But that's not all, Garrett. I think I was drugged. If Bridgette hadn't come along, he might have killed me."

"How could someone drug you?"

Tears pooled in her eyes. "Judge Warren brought me a plate of brownies. I had one before this whole incident happened."

"Judge Warren? Why would he want to drug you?"

"I don't know, but I don't see how else it could have happened."

Guilt rushed through him. He should have been there to protect her.

Vince knocked on the door and entered. "I'm glad you're here, Garrett." He glanced at Ashlynn. "How are you feeling?"

"I'm okay," she said, but her voice was small and weak.

"Did you find out who did this?" Garrett demanded.

Vince shook his head. "I've spoken with several of the people in the office at the time. No one saw anything."

Garrett sighed wearily. "How could they not see anyone?"

"It's a busy office and people are always coming and going. They don't have security cameras in the offices but they have them on the front doors. We'll search through the footage, but honestly we don't have a clue who we're looking for."

Ashlynn shook her head. "I didn't get a good look at him. He had that same mask covering his face as before. I grabbed it."

"No one saw a man in a mask, but that's easy to pull off and stuff into your pocket. We were able to get fiber samples from under your nails. They might provide some information. I also spoke with your assistant. She claims she also ate one of the brownies the judge brought you and nothing happened to her."

Ashlynn nodded, obviously thinking back. "Yes, she did have one. I watched her eat it."

"She also said she brought you coffee. The drugs could have been in that."

"Do you think Bridgette is the one who tried to drug me?" Ashlynn asked.

Garrett shook his head. "That's not likely. If Bridgette was the one drugging you, she could have easily told the police that the brownies made her sleepy, too. That would have focused suspicion away from her."

"True, and it was definitely a man who attacked me in the break room and Bridgette is the one who spooked him. And I can't think of one reason why Bridgette— or Judge Warren, either, for that matter—would want to kill me."

Vince glanced at Ashlynn. "Well, we'll follow up with Judge Warren and we're also having the remaining brownies and your coffee mug, what's left of it anyway, analyzed, but those will both take some time. Meanwhile, I'll have an officer posted at your door."

"That won't be necessary," she said. "They're releasing me soon. My injuries aren't that serious."

"And I'll be here until she's released," Garrett said. He wasn't leaving her unprotected again.

Vince nodded. "I'll let you know if we have any further questions," he told Ashlynn, then he walked out.

Garrett looked at her. "I shouldn't have left you."

"No, you had to focus on Jacob. Did you find out anything?"

"Not yet, but I'm not giving up. I don't want to leave you unprotected again, though. I'll phone Josh and see if I can drop you off at his place. You'll be safe there for the rest of the afternoon and it'll give you time to rest up. Don't worry. I trust him. He won't let anything happen to you."

"Are you sure he won't mind?"

"I'll call him but I know he won't. He does private security for an international company so if he's not off on an assignment he generally works from home."

"Fine, but I'd like to stop by my office first. I was going through my case files. I can pick them up and continue while I'm at Josh's."

"Ashlynn, you're supposed to be resting. You were nearly killed."

"Maybe you're right, but Jacob is still missing and I won't get any rest until he's home."

He had no choice but to agree, knowing she wasn't going to sit back and do nothing while her son...while their son...was missing. Wow, he still couldn't wrap his brain around the notion that he had a son.

He made the call to Josh and confirmed that, yes, he would be home and, no, he didn't mind one bit keeping an eye on Ashlynn for a while. Garrett stayed with her while the nurse finished the discharge paperwork and removed the IV.

Finally they left the hospital and drove downtown, back to the DA's offices. Ashlynn was pale as he parked and cut off the engine.

He gently touched her arm. "Are you sure you want to go back in there?" He hadn't considered how going back into the office where she'd been attacked would affect her, and by the ashen tone of her skin he doubted she had, either.

"I can run upstairs and get the files. Or, better yet, have someone bring them down."

"No," she said doggedly, unbuckling the seatbelt and jutting out that determined chin. "I'm going. I won't be terrorized this way."

He grinned at her stubbornness. When it didn't infuriate him, it made him proud.

Garrett walked with her to her office where she loaded the stack of files she'd requested into a box.

She was stuffing a few more, along with her notepad and pens, into the box when she turned and saw him staring at the photo of Jacob on her desk. He picked it up and outlined Jacob's image with his finger.

"He has my eyes," Garrett noted, his voice cracking with unguarded emotion.

"I know. You can't imagine how confusing it is to love someone so much who reminds you of someone—" She stopped herself. She'd been about to say "someone who'd let you down so much," but she realized how that would hurt him.

But she hadn't caught herself in time. "Someone you hate?"

"I don't hate you, Garrett. I never did. Even when I thought you'd rejected us, I couldn't hate you." She placed a comforting hand on his arm.

He covered her hand with his own, then replaced the photo on the desk and moved his hands to her face, softly caressing her cheeks. "I know I've let you and Jacob down before, Ashlynn, but I promise you, I won't rest until I bring Jacob home."

She stared up into his eyes. She saw a man where she used to see a boy and she saw determination and grit and…something else. A vulnerability she recognized. His finger stroked her lips and she saw him glance at her mouth as he drew nearer to her. Her heart jumped a beat. Was he going to kiss her? And what would she do if he tried?

She couldn't deny there was still such an attraction between them and she couldn't stop herself from remembering the safety of his arms embracing her. He'd always been her rock of strength and faith.

But then the cold reality hit her.

He hadn't always been her rock.

He felt the change in her too and backed away.

She shook her head. "I'm sorry, but I can't. How can I allow myself to fall for you when I can't trust you to stick around? I loved you so much, Garrett, and you shattered me. I can't go through that again. Besides, I need you to put Jacob front and center now."

He nodded and stepped away from her, but she saw the pain in his eyes at her rejection. She didn't really want to hurt him, especially now that she knew he hadn't meant to hurt her, but she had to keep her focus. She couldn't lose herself in Garrett again. She had Jacob now and she had to protect him. He'd already lost so much.

Garrett walked over to the box of files. "Is this everything?"

"Yes, for now."

He picked it up. She noticed how his muscles contracted beneath his shirt and felt a sigh of regret for what might have been.

* * *

They were back at Garrett's truck when Ken approached them with a file. "I'm glad I caught you," he said. "I didn't want to talk inside. Judge Warren checks out. He has no outstanding debts, no family connections with legal troubles. In fact, he's set to retire from the bench in a few months. He and his wife are planning to travel once he's retired. He seemed shook up when he learned what had happened to you and he was adamant that the brownies were not drugged. I think he was kind of hurt that anyone would even suggest it."

Ashlynn shook her head. "I have a hard time believing Judge Warren would try to harm me. He's my mentor. He's been like a second father to me all these years. I should talk to him and apologize."

Garrett nodded, but she could see he was more anxious to question the judge than apologize.

"What about Bridgette?" Garrett asked. "She brought you the coffee."

"Yes, and she's brought me coffee many times before. She's never drugged it previously. Besides, she wasn't the one who attacked me. In fact, she probably saved my life. And why would she want to hurt me?"

Ken ventured a guess. "Could be jealousy."

"Over what?"

"Everyone in the office knows Bridgette and her husband have been trying to have a baby and can't. Maybe she snapped and decided she would just take yours. It's possible she's obsessed. She snatches Jacob and then tries to kill you to get you out of the way. Jealousy has a way of making normally rational people do things you would never believe."

"That's ludicrous. Lots of people can't have children. That doesn't mean they're willing to resort to murder and abduction in order to become parents. There are other ways to have a child. Adoption, for instance."

Ken shook his head. "Maybe but not for former drug addicts. This is the reason I didn't want to talk inside the office. I ran a background on Bridgette's husband, Bruce. He spent six years in prison on drug charges and burglary. No agency is going to give someone with his background a child."

Garrett seemed excited about this new bit of information, but Ashlynn shook her head, dismayed. "I never knew that about her husband, but that still doesn't mean she's behind this. I find that very hard to believe. She's been a loyal friend to me."

Ken put away the files. "Well, I turned over what I discovered to the police so they can follow up on it."

"Ashlynn, we can't discount these incidents," Garrett said. "Whoever drugged you was nearby. No one saw anyone suspicious in your office or around your car when the bomb was set. Don't you see? Whoever is behind this is someone who can get close without raising suspicion. This person, or people, are targeting you. They have Jacob and now they want you out of the way. We can't just discount people because of an emotional connection. We have to follow up on every angle."

"Wouldn't I know if someone close to me was trying to kill me? Or wanted to take my son?"

"Not necessarily. Betrayal hurts so much because it is someone you trusted not to betray you."

She saw something in his face and got the idea he knew a thing or two about betrayal. Well, so did she because she'd been betrayed by him. She bit back that comment. He didn't need that reminder and it would only be cruel to bring it up again. She had to focus on the fact that he hadn't intentionally abandoned his family. He hadn't known about Jacob when he'd ended things with her. She needed to believe that because it helped to ease the sting of rejection.

Josh greeted them both then ushered Ashlynn into the den where she would have privacy while she sorted through her files but where he could also keep an eye on her.

Garrett shook his hand. "Thanks for doing this. I shouldn't have left her alone in her office, but I thought she would be safe there." He grimaced. "I was wrong."

"Not a problem," Josh assured him.

"If I text you a few names, can you do some background work on them?" He was starting with those in Ashlynn's inner circle—her ex-husband and her co-workers, including the DA and several of the police officers she worked closely with. "Her nanny was also killed. I would be inclined to think this was about her if Ashlynn's ex-husband hadn't been killed, as well. Someone is targeting her. I need to find out who."

Josh nodded, understanding. He knew about betrayal, having discovered his friend was behind his niece's abduction and a human trafficking ring operating out of their hometown. "Consider it done. Levi is coming into town tomorrow for an appointment at the neurologist. Want me to pull him in, too?"

Garrett nodded. "I'm hoping this will all be over and done with quickly, but I wouldn't mind having you both on alert in case I need backup."

"I'm here if you need me," Josh told him.

Garrett thanked him, said his goodbyes to Ashlynn and turned to leave.

I'm here if you need me. Garrett had known he could count on Josh to be there for him. It was one of the great things about having a band of brothers he trusted completely. He would always be there for them if they needed him and he could count on them to be there for him. Having that kind of backup was one of the reasons he'd decided to end his solitary lifestyle and return to life among people. He'd been in too many situations where he'd gotten in too deep and no one had had his back. He'd had to fight and claw and too many times shoot his way out of trouble.

He'd been shot, stabbed, beaten and even poisoned once, and each time he'd struggled with knowing he was alone in the world with only his determination and skill to protect him. They had protected him and they'd brought him home each time he'd rushed headlong into peril, but more and more the times between assignments had begun to feel more like loneliness than solitude. It was a feeling he doubted any of his ranger brothers understood. He knew they worried about him and his willingness and determination to find danger.

The doctors he'd seen had called it survivor's guilt

and assured him it would eventually eat him alive or get him killed if he didn't deal with it. They'd surely been right and even though he was still plagued by the feeling that he shouldn't have walked out of that ambush alive, he didn't want to nurse it alone any longer.

Now, with Ashlynn in trouble and his son—*his son*—missing, he was more pleased than ever before that he had the backup of the rangers on his side.

SIX

Years ago when Garrett had been a dumb kid working the streets, Mike Webb's chop shop had been housed on Raymond Street. He started there but was unsurprised to find the building had been torn down. The very nature of Mike's business meant he had to relocate often. But there had been a few meeting points, places where people would go to be found. Usually it was to buy drugs, a pastime he'd never ventured into, thankfully, but they were also places where someone could find information.

Garrett drove to several of those places and posed questions to people he encountered, but he saw no one he recognized. The players were all young kids and they either didn't know the names he dropped or were playing dumb. He figured it was probably the latter. They didn't know him from Adam and they weren't giving out details to strangers.

He sighed as he got back into his car. This was another dead end, just as Ashlynn had predicted. He hated most that he'd let her down again. She'd acted as if she hadn't been too optimistic about this panning out but he'd seen a glimmer of hope in her eyes and he disliked dashing that.

There had to be some way to reconnect with his old crew, aside from just parking his truck with the doors open and yelling at the top of his lungs that he was leaving the keys inside, then waiting to see who showed up. Although he would be willing to do that if he thought it would help him find Jacob.

He was definitely feeling the pressure as the hours passed with no ransom demand and no leads. He would do whatever it took to bring Jacob home. He wanted to get to know his son and have the opportunity to be a dad. He'd grown up without a father and now that Stephen was dead, Jacob could be looking at the same kind of future. Garrett didn't want that for him. He'd never thought about being a father, but now that he knew he was, he wanted to be a part of his child's life. But first he had to find Jacob and bring him home safely.

He tried three more spots where his old crew used to hang out but still made no headway. Things had changed too much in town in the years since he'd been gone. And more than just the town was different. He was, too. He'd once been at home here, but he wasn't that same dumb kid who used to steal cars for Mike Webb for a hundred bucks a pop. He'd made it out of this neighborhood. The army had cleaned him up and given him a skill and a purpose.

He glanced around and spotted mostly young kids on the streets. This was why he'd accepted when his friend from church had asked him to volunteer to men-

tor inner city kids. He had something to offer them—
hope that if he could make it out, they could, as well.
And speaking of his mentoring…

He spotted a familiar face walking along Harris
Street—Adam Greer, the boy he'd been at the courthouse to support yesterday when he'd run into Ashlynn.
He didn't even know what had happened in Adam's
mother's case. Adam stopped at the corner and Garrett
saw him push a bill into another boy's hand and accept
something that he quickly shoved into his pocket.

He sighed, disappointed. Adam's mother was a drug
addict. Was he buying for her or following in her footsteps? Either way, Garrett couldn't sit back and allow it
to happen. He threw his truck into gear and roared up
the road, stopping in front of Adam and jumping out.

"Mr. G., what are you doing here?" the boy asked,
using the nickname they'd given him, forgetting that
Garrett was his first, not his last name. He'd gotten
that sort of confusion his entire life.

"I saw that drug buy, Adam." He pulled open the
passenger door. "Get in. Let's have a talk."

Ashlynn set down the file she was reviewing and
sighed. Nothing had turned up that might be related to
her son's disappearance and she was becoming more
and more certain it had nothing to do with one of her
past cases.

She took a break and stood from her spot curled up
on the sofa in Josh and Elise's living room. Placing
her file on the coffee table, she stretched her arms and
legs. There were photographs on the fireplace mantel,

including one of Josh and a teenage girl who must be the niece Garrett had mentioned before. She also spotted a picture of a group of men in uniform and picked it up, thinking this must be Josh and Garrett's ranger team. Searching the group she found Garrett kneeling on the front row.

Someone cleared his throat behind her, and she realized she'd been caught snooping. She turned and saw Josh standing at the doorway.

"I'm sorry," she said, replacing the photograph.

"It's okay," he told her. He walked in and motioned toward the image. "That was our team before the ambush." He glanced at her curiously. "Did Garrett tell you about that?"

"He did mention it." Actually, he'd done his best to skim over the details of the event that had ripped their relationship apart.

"Only six of us made it out that night." He pointed to each man as he said their names. "Matt, Levi, Colton, Blake, Garrett and me." He pointed to a tall, lanky redhead. "That was Marcus, Garrett's best friend. Has he mentioned him?"

She shook her head but wasn't surprised since Josh had already told her the rest of these men hadn't survived the ambush. She looked at the wedding photo of Josh and Elise next to the photo of the rangers and felt a pang of jealousy. They'd gotten their happy ending. "Did you know about my engagement to Garrett?"

He nodded. "Yes, we knew. When he rejoined the group after that leave, you were all he talked about. He was crazy in love with you, Ashlynn." Josh stuffed his hands into his pockets and looked weary. "We all lost so much that night. We each dealt with it in our own ways. Garrett ran from it. He took off and I didn't even see or hear from him for months. He just lost himself. But one thing he never lost was his devotion to the rangers. Whenever any one of us has needed him, he's been there."

She sighed. That statement did not make her feel any better. He could be devoted to his friends but not to his family. "He wasn't there for me when I needed him."

"I know he let you down, but you have to know that's not who he is. That was a bad time in his life and he messed up. You're having a hard time trusting him and I get that. When I first met Elise, I didn't trust anyone. I didn't want to depend on another person because I was afraid of being disappointed."

"How did she change your mind?"

His lips twitched into a smile. "She didn't. God changed me and because He did I was able to let Elise inside. All I'm saying is that I know what it's like to step out on a limb without knowing if you're going to fall or not. But I also know Garrett cares for you. I think he probably never stopped caring about you."

She was suddenly uncomfortable with the direction this conversation was going. Of course he would stand up for his friend, but he didn't understand how badly she'd been hurt or how frightened she was that Garrett would leave her again. She just couldn't take that chance on him. "I'm trusting Garrett to find Jacob because I really have no other choice. But I can't trust him with anything else, not now, maybe not ever."

His phone buzzed and he pulled it out and glanced at the screen. "It's Garrett. He's pulling into the driveway."

She hurried to the door to wait for him, anxious to know if he'd found anything that might help lead them to Jacob. She watched his truck pull into the garage and he got out a moment later.

"Well?" she asked before he even made it inside. "Were your old contacts able to offer any information?"

He shook his head. "No, my old contacts were a bust. However—" he opened the passenger door and grabbed the arm of a young boy, pulling him from the car "—my new contact might just be able to offer us some information. Ashlynn, meet Adam Greer, my mentee."

Adam was just a young kid who appeared nervous as Garrett stood over him. He plopped down in a chair and spent five minutes staring at the floor.

"I caught him buying drugs for his mom downtown. Despite the fact that she was just convicted yesterday and given a year's probation, she talked her sixteen-year-old son into scoring some junk for her."

Adam flushed with embarrassment as Garrett continued.

"We started doing some talking and it turns out Adam has an idea where Mike Webb's shop might be."

"How would he know that?" Ashlynn asked.

The boy glanced up at her. "My mom and her boyfriend used to steal cars for Mike in order to get money for drugs. She called me to pick her up there once even though I didn't have a license at the time or a car. I had a friend drive me over there. That was only about six months ago."

Garrett nodded. "We drove by the place, and I'm sure I saw a white van parked out back. It could be our van. It's worth checking out, don't you think?"

"Absolutely. We should take a look." She glanced at Adam. "Thank you for helping us."

He shrugged. "Mr. G. told me about your son. My mom has been in and out of jail my whole life so I know what it's like to grow up without a mama. Your boy should be happy to have one that cares about him."

She saw pain on his young face and remembered Garrett telling her yesterday—was it really only yesterday this all began?—that Adam had been at the courthouse to see his mother who was addicted to drugs. She didn't have to wonder what kind of turmoil he'd lived in. She knew it firsthand, and she felt bad for him. He was fortunate that Garrett arrived in his life to help guide him.

"I'm not anxious to take down old friends," Garrett said, "but if Mike's at all connected to Jacob's kidnapping, I won't hesitate. Our son is more important to me than old loyalties."

It warmed her heart to hear his proclamation. She saw him glance at Josh, whose eyebrows were raised in surprise. He obviously hadn't heard the news about Jacob and Garrett's connection.

He grinned at Josh and nodded. "You heard right. Jacob is my son."

"What are you going to do with him?" she asked, motioning toward Adam.

"I'll phone my friend Dave, the one who suggested I be a mentor, and ask him to come get him."

"So, what do we do now?" she asked. "I doubt we can obtain a search warrant based on just a generic white van."

He shook his head. "It'll be dark soon. I say we wait a few hours then go by his place and do some reconnaissance work of our own. If we see the van and can determine it's the one involved in Jacob's abduction, then we'll call in Vince and the police."

She nodded but she couldn't hide the expression of worry on her face. Could she stand one more lead not panning out? What if nothing came of it? Then they'd have wasted precious time in finding Jacob.

Another thought occurred to her. "Won't there be security?"

"I'll bring my tools, just in case, but Mike never trusted security systems. He knows too many hackers to believe in secure. He had some guard dogs six years ago, but mostly he just relied on his own reputation to deter thieves. No one wanted to cross him. I'm hoping that's still the way he operates."

"Yet we're going to cross him."

"Not unless he's involved in this someway. Don't worry, we'll be careful." Garrett squeezed her shoulder reassuringly. "We will find him, Ash. We'll bring him home."

He pulled her into his embrace and she went willingly, finding comfort in his strong arms and solid chest. He made her feel safe and reassured, and she longed to lose herself here and not have to face the cold realities of life.

She closed her eyes, breathed in the musky scent of Garrett's aftershave and found herself lifting a silent prayer that God would be on their side. She didn't know if it would help, but at this point, she was willing to try anything.

The street was nearly deserted when Garrett parked his car across from Mike's shop. It was a simple large warehouse with a fence surrounding the perimeter. Inside the fence were car parts and pieces of vehicles. It looked like a mini junkyard. Garrett was trained to infiltrate compounds and he'd used his ranger training many times to rescue hostages. Breaking in wouldn't be a problem. The real problem would be convincing Ashlynn to stay in the car. One glance at her and he knew that wasn't going to happen. He hadn't been able to convince her to stay back at Josh's house and he instinctively knew she wasn't going to stay in the car, either. All he could do was make the best of it and watch her back. Still, he couldn't resist one more try.

"Are you sure you want to do this?" he asked her. "I can see the headline now. ADA Arrested for Breaking and Entering."

She flashed him a determined look and that chin jutted out again. "I'm going."

"Fine. But I'm going to walk the perimeter alone first. I'll see if I can locate the van. It was parked out back earlier. Let's just hope it's not inside the shop being stripped of its parts. I'll also look for vulnerable points in the fence." He opened the door but she grabbed his arm, stopping him, her face full of doubt and mistrust.

"Don't you go in without me, Garrett."

"I'll be right back," he assured her.

He got out and hurried across the street while she scrunched down in her seat so as not to be seen. He suspected she wouldn't stay down long before she peeked out to see what was happening.

Walking along the east and west sides, he found two decent entry points. He was about to head back to the car when he noticed something in the lot. He reached for his compact binoculars and zoomed in, spotting the white van parked behind the shop near the back door. Its parts were still intact. He doubted that would be the case in a few hours.

He reached into another pocket for his pliers and knelt down, quickly cutting into the fence and feeling only slightly guilty at not keeping his word to Ashlynn. He tried to tell himself that she wasn't trained for this, and it was true, but mostly he wanted to keep her out of danger. If anyone walked out of that shop and spotted him, it would be game over. He knew from firsthand experience that Mike Webb was a dangerous man. He didn't want Ashlynn anywhere near him.

Garrett slipped through the fence and moved silently to the back of the building. Noises from inside indicated they were working, probably chopping cars. He imagined Ashlynn angrily fussing at him in the car for continuing on without her, but then he doubted she could see him from her vantage point.

Moving toward the back of the van, he opened the door softly. He didn't know exactly what he was looking for to indicate this was the same van from the security feed, but he didn't have to wonder long. His gut clenched when on the back floorboard he spotted a small stuffed bunny. Business vans didn't have children's stuffed toys in the back of them.

He grabbed the bunny, his heart breaking at the thought that not only had Jacob likely been inside this van, he'd been taken out without his stuffed animal for security. Had he cried for his lost friend and was he crying now for his mother? Garrett's blood boiled at the thought that whoever had him had been so careless with Jacob's needs. He was determined they would pay.

God, please comfort Jacob and keep him safe until we bring him home.

He tucked the bunny into his jacket and softly closed the door. All he had to do now was make it back to the fence and to the car; then they could alert Vince that they'd located the van and let the police swoop in and recover it.

But he froze when he spotted Ashlynn slipping through the hole he'd cut into the fence. His heart dropped and fear rushed through him. What did she think she was doing?

He motioned for her to get back, but she obviously couldn't see him.

His heart raced at the notion that any one of those men inside could step out and spot her and then she would be in danger. He pulled his gun and headed her way, praying he could get her out of here in time.

She'd obviously spotted him crouched against the side of the building and changed her direction, moving toward him despite his signaling for her to get back. But Ashlynn froze mid-step when the door to the shop opened and someone stepped outside.

"Who are you?" a male voice asked.

Garrett didn't recognize the voice. He had to stop this guy before he called out for his friends.

Garrett leaped up, grabbed the guy's shoulder and rammed the gun into his back. "Don't say a word," he commanded in a hard, hushed voice. Ashlynn relaxed as the man lifted his hands and followed Garrett's prompting.

She hurried past the door and joined Garrett. "What are you going to do with him?" she asked, her voice also low.

"The only thing I can." He reached into his pocket and slipped her the keys. "Go back to the car and start the engine and be ready to get out of here. I'll be right behind you."

She nodded and turned, quietly heading back. He watched her climb through the fence.

The man shook his head and chuckled. "Fella, you don't know who you're messing with. Do you have any idea whose place this is you're robbing?"

"I'm not robbing anyone. I was just checking something out."

"This isn't a library. These cars belong to Mike Webb. Heard of him? He'll kill you and your girl for breaking in here."

"I think Mike is about to have his hands full with

something else," Garrett said, pressing the man hard against the outside wall. "Like kidnapping a little kid."

"What? Mike ain't into kidnapping kids. He's no pervert."

Garrett pulled the bunny from his jacket. "Oh, yeah? Then why did I find this inside the white van parked behind the shop? Who does this belong to?"

The man looked at the stuffed figure then swore under his breath. "We just got that van in today. We didn't have nothing to do with a kidnapping."

"Who brought the van in?"

"A guy named Meeks. Randy Meeks. He's not a regular, but Mike buys cars off him from time to time. Look fella, I don't want any part of a kidnapping."

Garrett stuffed the bunny back into his coat. He spotted Ashlynn back at the car and knew he couldn't wait much longer. Soon this guy's friends would come looking for him. "I appreciate your help," he said before slamming his gun into the back of his head. The guy uttered an *oof* then slipped down the side of the building. He would have a headache when he awoke, and he would certainly spill what he knew about Garrett and Ashlynn's visit to Mike. They needed to get back to the precinct so Vince could arrange for the task force to raid this shop before these guys cleaned it out.

He hurried back to the car and slipped into the driver's seat. Ashlynn had the engine running and he quickly took off. Ideally, he would stick around and watch the place, making sure they didn't start hauling things away, but he couldn't risk that, not with Ashlynn beside him.

He dialed Vince as he drove and updated him on what they'd found. Vince assured him he would have a team ready to raid the warehouse within the hour. When he was certain they weren't being followed, Garrett pulled over the car and got out, slamming the door hard. "What were you thinking?" he demanded, turning to Ashlynn, who got out from the other side and walked around the car. "Why did you follow me? You could have been killed."

She shrank back at his angry tone then jutted out her chin in defiance. "You promised you'd be right back but you went in by yourself anyway. What were you doing?"

"I did what I had to do."

"I knew I shouldn't have trusted you."

He hated the way she hissed out those words, but he didn't back down. What she'd done hadn't been smart. "I didn't want you to get hurt, Ash."

"You don't get to decide that for me, Garrett. I'm a grown woman and a prosecutor. I can make my own decisions." She huffed away and folded her arms angrily over her chest, but after a moment turned back to him. "What did you find?"

He sighed. He wanted to be angry with her because she had been reckless but also because it put off having to show her. He pulled the bunny from his jacket. When she saw it, her eyes widened and her chin quivered. He hated that look. It cut him to his core and he vowed he wouldn't rest until he could wipe it away.

"Wh-where did you get that? That's Jacob's bunny."

"It was inside the van."

She took it from his outstretched hand and hugged it to her chest. When she looked at him, her eyes were knowing and determined.

"He was inside that van."

Garrett nodded, then pulled her into his arms as tears slipped down her face. His own emotions were threatening to burst through him. "We'll find him," he told her, doing his best to reassure them both.

They turned around and drove back to watch the warehouse to make certain the men inside didn't move the van before Vince and his team showed up. She shouldn't have been so hard on him. Ashlynn knew that, but she was still angry that he'd left her behind. He'd promised to come right back, but he'd broken that promise and gone into the compound alone. Yes, she knew it had been reckless to follow him, but she'd just been so mad. But when she remembered the man's surprised expression when he'd stepped outside and the fear that had gushed through her, she knew she'd truly messed up. If Garrett hadn't been there, this man could have hurt her and she would never find out what had happened to Jacob. She was thankful for Garrett's intervention, but it still burned her that he'd broken his word to her...again.

The police finally arrived and stormed inside. The group had obviously been alerted by the man who'd discovered her that they were in trouble, because they looked as if they were preparing to clear out. They were boxing up car parts for shipping and stripping the remaining cars inside. Several of the men tried to run but were quickly caught and returned.

Once the shop was secured, Ashlynn walked with Vince and Garrett to the van outside. Vince pulled open the door and peered inside before shutting it and turning back to them. "I've got a team waiting to tow this van back to the station for processing." His eyes blazed with excitement. His team had just taken a chunk out of the car theft ring plaguing the city and he was one step closer to finding a kidnapped child. It was a good night for him in a professional sense.

As the police secured the scene, Ashlynn noticed Garrett looking around. He appeared agitated and angry. Finally she walked to him and placed her hand on his arm.

"You okay?"

He nodded but sighed wearily. "I was just thinking about that guy who walked out of the shop. That was me once upon a time. I look around at all of this and I realize how amazing it is that I made it. I found a way out of here, but most of those kids I grew up in foster care with never did. What kind of future does Adam have with a drug-addicted mother who has him already buying her drugs for him?"

"He has you," she said admiringly. "He could use a good role model."

He looked at her, his green eyes blazing through her. "You have to know this wasn't the future I planned, Ashlynn. I would never have abandoned you and Jacob. I made a vow to myself that I wouldn't be that kind of dad. I never wanted my son to live without his father."

She nodded. "I understand that, but it happened and I can't forget that. Judge Warren used to tell me that you can tell a person by his actions, not by his words. That's how I try to live my life now. I've opened up my heart too many times and had it broken. I won't take that risk again, especially not with Jacob's heart."

He pushed back a strand of hair from her face and pressed it behind her ear. "I've thought about you every day since that night I left you. You never left my thoughts no matter how hard I tried to push you out of them." He shrugged. "I was dumb and I made a mistake that I can't undo. But I want you to know how sorry I am, Ash. I let you down and I hate that I'm one of those people you place in that category."

She struggled to hold back the tears as they walked to his truck and got inside. She hated it, too, and wished more than anything she could learn to trust him again.

While the van was being processed, Garrett and Ashlynn returned to the police station so Garrett could use the police database to look up the name the guy they'd encountered had given him—Randy Meeks.

It didn't take him long to find a file under that name. "Looks like Meeks is no stranger to the criminal justice system. He's been arrested for business burglary, assault and robbery."

"And soon to be added—kidnapping," Ashlynn said as she looked over Garrett's shoulder at the extensive list. His mug shot revealed a small-statured man with beady, dark eyes.

"Do you recognize him?" Garrett asked.

She shook her head. She'd never seen him before.

"Well, he can't be the man who attacked you. He's only five foot six. But he could be working with him."

"I've been through my files. I've never prosecuted this man."

Garrett scrolled through the file onscreen to the last known address then frowned. "The only address on file for him is listed as invalid." He slammed his hand on the desk in frustration. "This guy is the key. I know he is."

"I'll phone Ken," Ashlynn said. "He has a knack for locating people who don't want to be found."

When he answered, she passed along the information they had and asked him to do what he could.

"Where did you say you got this guy's name?"

"A chop shop in the west part of town where we found the van that might have been used in Jacob's kidnapping. One of the men working there told Garrett a guy named Randy Meeks had brought it in. We have to track him down. He could be the key to finding Jacob."

"Ashlynn, he could have been lying about the guy who brought in the van."

"Maybe, but he gave us a name and that name belongs to a real person. Just do what you can, Ken."

"All right. Let me do some research on this guy," Ken said. "I'll get back to you when I know something."

She clicked off the call and looked at Garrett. "He doesn't seem very hopeful about finding him."

"He will," Garrett assured her. "And if he doesn't then we'll find another lead to the kidnappers. We're not giving up, Ashlynn. We will find Jacob and bring him home."

She was grateful once again for his strength and assuredness. It was the only thing getting her through this nightmare. And no matter how she tried to fight it, she found herself believing in him, trusting him. She was still a long way away from allowing him to become a permanent part of their lives, but it was nice start.

Early the next morning, Garrett received a call from Vince with the preliminary lab results on the brownies. He listened, then hung up and turned to her.

Ashlynn held her breath, waiting to hear. These results could mean she'd been betrayed by her own mentor and someone she considered a dear friend.

Garrett looked at her. "Preliminary results found no drugs in the brownies."

She breathed a sigh of relief and only then realized how nervous she'd been, believing the judge could have been involved. Then she remembered Ken's words about how hurt Judge Warren had been at the accusation.

"I should go apologize to him," she said. "I shouldn't have doubted him."

Garrett nodded. "We'll go, but this doesn't completely exonerate him, Ashlynn. These are only preliminary results. We still need to be careful who we trust."

Garrett drove, and as they approached the house of Judge Warren, Ashlynn tensed. This man was her mentor and her long-time friend. But the closer she came to facing him, the more she remembered Garrett's warning that the killer had to be someone close to her. She was glad Garrett was beside her as they walked up the front steps and rang the bell, even though she knew he had different reasons for wanting to come. As he had with Stephen, he wanted to look the man in the eye to ascertain for himself whether or not he was involved.

Judge Warren opened the door. His usual cheerful smile vanished when he saw her and she hated to see that change.

"Ashlynn, I see you brought your bodyguard with you," he said, glancing behind her to Garrett. "What can I do for you?" She cringed at his icy tone.

"I was hoping we could talk," she said.

He opened the door wider and motioned them inside, then led them into a den and offered them both a seat. "I would offer you something to eat or drink, but…" He trailed off, his point made.

Ashlynn felt her face warm at his hurt tone. She'd known him too long to believe him capable of any kind of deceit, much less kidnapping and murder. However, her son's life was at stake and she couldn't rely on her feelings to guide her even in this matter.

"A wise man once told me that a good prosecutor couldn't allow emotion to guide her thinking. It was good advice. And even though my regard for you tells me absolutely that you weren't involved in this, I still had to consider the possibility." She hoped he could see the pleading look in her eye and hear the apologetic tone of her voice. She didn't want to accuse him.

He sighed knowingly and nodded. "You're right.

I'm just a silly old man wearing my feelings on my sleeve. Of course, I had nothing to do with drugging you, Ashlynn. I brought those brownies to your office for the same reason I've brought them many times before, just to be friendly." He glanced toward the kitchen where she assumed his wife was. "Also, because ever since my wife retired from teaching, she bakes all day long and if I ate everything she made, I'd be as big as the side of a house. That's why I started sharing her goodies with friends."

Ashlynn nodded, relieved by the honesty she saw in him. "My assistant ate one of your brownies, too, and nothing happened to her so we had pretty much discounted the fact that the drugs were in the brownies. This morning we learned lab results appear to corroborate that."

"But you still had to investigate the possibility. I confess, I wasn't thrilled to be interrogated by the police. I'm too used to being on the other side of the table." He reached out and took her hands in his. "But I do understand."

Mrs. Warren appeared at the doorway wiping her hands on her apron. "Charles, I wasn't aware we had company. You should have come and told me. Hello, Ashlynn."

"Hello, Mrs. Warren. How are you?"

"I'm doing well." She approached Garrett and held out her hand. "Alicia Warren."

He shook her outstretched hand. "Garrett Lewis."

"Ashlynn is here asking about an incident that happened at her office and Mr. Lewis accompanied her."

Mrs. Warren gave a sympathetic look. "Yes, I heard about your son, Ashlynn. I'm so sorry. Have there been any leads?"

"We're following up on several," Garrett commented, "but nothing concrete yet."

"That's terrible. Can I get either of you something to drink or eat?"

Ashlynn saw Judge Warren's eyes widen. He obviously hadn't told his wife about the police's accusations about her brownies. Ashlynn figured he'd wanted to spare her feelings. But there was no way she would ever eat another brownie again.

"Thank you for the offer," Garrett said, "but we've got to be going."

She was grateful for his tactful response.

They said their goodbyes and Judge Warren walked them to the front door.

"I do hope the police find your son, Ashlynn."

She smiled at his sincerity and thanked him.

As they walked to the car, Garrett glanced her way. "What did you think?"

"I hate hurting him. He was always so good to me. He was my mentor, Garrett. I find it difficult to believe he had a hand in this."

Garrett shrugged. "Vince's interview with him didn't raise any flags and given the lab results, I think it's safe to say he wasn't involved."

"I hope you're right. I would hate to think someone so close to me would do something so terrible."

But if Judge Warren wasn't responsible for Jacob's kidnapping, then who had her son?

* * *

By that afternoon, Ken managed to track down an address for Randy Meeks and Ashlynn was thankful he was on their side. Even Garrett confessed that he was impressed with Ken's abilities. He drove to the address Ken had given them. It was a run-down apartment building on the west side of town. Ashlynn was glad Garrett was by her side. They took the steps to the second floor and Garrett pulled his gun. He pounded on the door and called for Meeks to open up.

When no one answered, he kicked in the door and burst inside. This was no time for niceties, not while a child was missing. The place was a mess, with clothes and food and garbage littering the floor. Ashlynn glanced around, part of her hoping Jacob wasn't being kept in such dirty conditions but also hoping he was here and she could take him home.

Garrett checked the rooms then holstered his gun. "No one is here."

Ashlynn pulled out her cell phone. "I'll have Ken run his financials to see if there's been any hits on credit cards. I also want to get a warrant for his cell phone records."

Garrett nodded his agreement. "I saw a group of kids in the parking lot. I think I'll go talk to them and see what they know about their neighbor Meeks. Maybe they have an idea where he might be."

She nodded and watched him walk out. As she waited for Ken to answer or his voicemail to pick up, she scanned the apartment, disgusted by the way in which Meeks lived. It took her back to her childhood days when she'd still lived with her father. His drinking binges had often left their home looking like this, although even then Ashlynn had done her best to try to tidy up. But she'd quickly learned to steer clear of him when he was drinking or face the brunt of his alcohol-fueled abuse. Cleanliness had taken a backseat to safety.

Ken's voicemail finally picked up and she left him a brief message explaining what she needed. She put away her phone and picked up a framed photograph from its spot on an end table. There was something familiar about the faces in the group photo.

Suddenly, the door slammed behind her. She turned and gasped as a man she recognized from his photo as Meeks lurched at her, clamping a sweaty hand over her mouth and a knife's blade to her throat.

SEVEN

The photo fell from her hand as Meeks pressed the knife deeper into her neck.

"Stop struggling," he commanded, pulling his arm tighter around her. His breath on her face was hot and menacing as he spoke. "You're looking for your little boy?" he hissed. "Well he's gone."

Panic gripped her. No, he couldn't be gone. This man was only trying to frighten and upset her. Couldn't he see the pleading in her eyes? Could he see how much she needed her baby back in her arms? He had to have some notion of a conscience, didn't he?

Garrett opened the door. Surprise when he saw them quickly turned to steely determination. He drew his gun as Meeks spotted him and pulled her closer, using Ashlynn as a shield.

"Drop it or I snap her neck," he hollered.

Ashlynn saw the result of all Garrett's years of training. He didn't flinch. He braced his arm, aiming his gun and moving inside the apartment. His jaw was set and his hands steady. "Let her go."

"I said drop it," Meeks demanded again, his snarl high pitched and uncertain compared to Garrett's calm, cool response.

"That's not going to happen."

Meeks tightened his grip, causing Ashlynn to cry out in pain as the knife dug into her neck.

"Okay, okay," Garrett said. He carefully placed his gun on the floor, his eyes never leaving Meeks. "There. I'm unarmed. Now, let her go."

"Why are you in my house?"

"We're looking for a child that was kidnapped yesterday afternoon. He was in the van you returned to Mike Webb's place."

"I didn't take no kid," Meeks insisted. "I just returned the van for a friend."

"That's a lie," Ashlynn cried. "You just told me he was gone."

"Shut up!" Meeks hollered, digging the knife in again and causing Ashlynn to cry out in pain.

But Garrett didn't react to her cry. He stood calmly, nodding, his hand on his hip. "I believe you. What's the name of the friend?"

"I'm not a snitch like those guys Webb has working for him. I don't inform on my friends."

"I admire your loyalty. But you see we have a problem because that's my friend you're threatening with a knife, and I'm also extremely loyal to my friends. We need to work something out here before anyone gets hurt."

He took another step into the room, but his voice never wavered. Ashlynn noticed the hand on his hip slowly moving toward his belt, then she spotted a flash of metal as Garrett slung something at Meeks.

He groaned and released her, grabbing his thigh and screaming out in pain. Ashlynn slipped through his grasp and out of the way as Garrett retrieved his gun from the floor and had Meeks in custody in what seemed like one fast movement.

Her heart was pounding and a lump of gratitude rose in her throat. Garrett hadn't allowed her to be hurt. He'd protected her, just as she'd instinctively known he would. A wave of thankfulness and grief overwhelmed her and she buried her face in her hands, unable to hold back the rush of emotion that enveloped her.

Garrett placed a hand on her shoulder and his voice was full of worry as he knelt beside her. "Are you okay?" She thought she heard a slight quiver in his voice but she dismissed it. Surely she'd imagined it. Based on what she'd just witnessed, nothing could frighten this man.

"I'm fine," she assured him, then took a deep breath and allowed him to pull her to her feet. She looked and saw Meeks tied up with what appeared to be the cords from the window blinds.

Garrett's hand was heavy on her shoulder. "Are you sure you're all right? He didn't hurt you?"

She heard that quiver again and looked up into his face. His brows were furrowed and worry pierced his eyes.

"Really I'm fine," she said again, this time resting her head on his shoulder. His arms tightened around her and she felt the rapid beat of his heart just beginning to slow. It was unbelievable to her that his heart could have been racing when he'd appeared so calm.

The thought hit her that, had Garrett not come back into the apartment, Meeks might have killed her and she would never see her son again. The realization that he'd played a part in kidnapping her son came blazing back to her, pushing away any residual fear she'd experienced from Meeks's attack.

She pulled from Garrett's arms and lunged at Meeks. "Where is my son?"

Garrett's arms tightened around her waist, preventing her from getting too close. The man sneered at her with his eyes but he didn't respond to her demand for answers.

Garrett pulled her aside and knelt in front of Meeks. "We're looking for the little boy you helped kidnap yesterday. Tell me where he is and it'll go easier on you."

"I don't know anything about kidnapping a boy."

"The van you sold to Mike Webb yesterday was used in an abduction and murder. Now, we know you're involved, and I'm certain you know the charges for kidnapping and murder can be steep. Help us out and help yourself out by telling us what you did with the boy."

He looked at Garrett then at Ashlynn and sneered again. "She doesn't deserve to be a mother."

His words dug into her soul deeper than any knife could stab her. The photo she'd received with the note came back to her. The similar words confirmed he'd sent it.

Garrett too seemed surprised by his words. "Why doesn't she deserve to be a mother? What's she done?"

He turned his glare from Ashlynn to Garrett. "I'm not saying another word. If you're arresting me, I want my lawyer. If not, untie me and get out of my house. This is unlawful imprisonment."

Garrett stood and faced her, then blew out a frustrated breath. "I'll call Vince." He touched her arm ever so slightly, almost a caress against her skin. She shivered but told herself it was less from his touch and more about the worry of the situation. Meeks knew where her son was and he wasn't talking. It was now nearing forty-eight hours since Jacob had been abducted. Were they running out of time to find him?

Garrett called for backup and soon had Meeks in a patrol car on his way to booking. Meeks still hadn't uttered a word about where Jacob was, but Garrett could tell he knew. What really shook him was Meeks's statement that Ashlynn didn't deserve to be a mother. His words mirrored the note that had been left on her desk. He had to be the one who sent it. Did he know her personally? Or was he some psycho who'd seen her on TV and decided women with high-powered careers didn't make good mothers?

She'd denied knowing him so that left psycho stalker. That meant Jacob could be anywhere.

When Vince arrived with his team, Garrett updated him on the situation. "We should start by uncovering any known associates of Meeks's. I also want a full detailed financial analysis to look for any anomalies."

"I'll call one of my officers back at the precinct and get them on that," Vince assured him.

He glanced over at Ashlynn on the phone, no doubt with Ken, giving him the same instructions, probably. She slipped her phone into her pocket then curled her arms across her chest. He knew she was trying to keep it together, but her breaking point was near. Meeks was the only lead they had right now and he was a good one. He hoped and prayed if they couldn't get Meeks talking that something would show up on his financials.

Garrett walked over and put his arms around her. She was shaking, fighting to hold herself together. She was trying to remain strong and she was one tough lady. Who else could have been through the past hours with the grace and strength she'd exhibited?

He didn't give any credence to what Meeks said, either. He couldn't imagine she wouldn't be an amazing mother. She'd always had a nurturing way about her. He wondered how many people had seen beneath that tough exterior to the generous and loving woman inside. Had Stephen seen that side of her? Few others would have, he decided. She wasn't one to let people get too close to her because she'd been brokenhearted too many times. With shame, he realized he'd caused her that same pain even though he'd been trying to do just the opposite and protect her.

Even though she was an ADA, she was also a victim, so Vince asked her not to touch anything. It could corrupt the chain of evidence that might be used against Meeks during a trial of kidnapping her child. Garrett was certain Vince would have preferred she wait outside or go back to the precinct, but Garrett was determined not to let her out of his sight again. He'd taken his eyes off her for only a few minutes and look what had nearly happened. He wasn't taking any more risks with her safety.

He took over the job of entering the evidence the team collected into a logbook, examining each item carefully first, while Ashlynn watched.

He picked up a framed photograph that looked old and worn. He turned it over and saw a group of kids together for a shot. It didn't look like a sports team or class photo, and nothing about it captured his attention. He wrote it in the log and turned to place it in a bin.

But Ashlynn grabbed his arm to stop him and stared at it, jogging his memory that it had been at her feet when Meeks was holding the knife to her. Had she been looking at it before the attack against her?

"What is it?" Garrett asked. "Do you recognize this photo?"

She nodded, but she'd turned a shade whiter. "I do." She stroked her hand over the image of the woman with the dark hair and wide smile. "I saw this before but I couldn't place where. Now, I remember. This woman in the back is Kathryn Rollins, my foster mother."

This time Garrett gaped. He took back the photo and stared at it. "Are you sure?"

"I could never forget her face. She tried to present a happy front to the world, but her eyes were cold and hard and so was she. Her hair is shorter in this picture, which is why I guess I didn't immediately recognize her." She pointed to another adult. "That's her husband. He was a wisp of a man who did whatever she commanded."

Now Garrett understood. Ashlynn had been in an abusive foster home before she'd come to the group facility where they'd first met. She'd been beaten severely by her foster mother and had later testified against her about the atrocities she'd suffered at the woman's hands. He looked down at the photo and the image. This was the woman who had caused Ashlynn so much pain and suffering. "This was your foster mother?"

This didn't make any sense. Why would Meeks steal an old photograph of Ashlynn from when she was a little girl? What would he possibly want with it? "When did you last see this photograph? Had you noticed it missing from your house?"

She shook her head. "No, this isn't my photograph. I had one similar to this but I tore it up and threw it into the fireplace years ago. I couldn't stand looking at the smug smile on her face and the happy image she tried so hard to portray to the world."

He stared at the photo again, trying to process this new information. If this wasn't Ashlynn's picture then it must belong to Meeks. Had one of these freckled-faced boys grown up to be Meeks? And if so, why had he targeted Ashlynn?

Somehow, they had to convince Meeks to talk. He was the key to figuring this all out.

Ashlynn watched through the two-way mirror as Vince questioned Meeks. She'd been in this spot many times in a professional capacity and each time she'd wanted the detectives to find that hot button that would get the suspect talking, but she had never wanted it more than she did now. She needed Meeks to talk. He was the crucial link to finding out where Jacob was being held and who was involved.

But Meeks remained tight-lipped. He claimed he knew nothing about the van in question and nothing about a kidnapping. Ashlynn tried to remain calm but inside she was screaming. The mother in her wanted to claw his eyes out until he told her where Jacob was. The prosecutor in her wanted to toss the book at him and send him away for years. Neither reaction would garner them the information they needed.

Vince exited the interview room, his expression full of disappointment. "He's not talking," Vince said.

She'd seen that for herself through the two-way mirror, but to hear Vince sound so defeated still bothered her. He didn't believe they would get Meeks to tell what he knew, meaning this lead was quickly drying up.

"He's definitely not the right build to be the man who was in your house," Garrett noted.

She shook her head. "Nor the man who attacked me in the break room. He's too skinny. Yet it seems too coincidental that we were in the same foster home." She still couldn't believe this all could have some connection to Kathryn Rollins. As far as she knew, the woman had died in prison so she surely couldn't be acting out a revenge scenario. Ashlynn took the file from Vince. "Let me speak to him."

"That's not a good idea," Vince cautioned.

"It's better than doing nothing." She opened the door and walked into the interview room before he could protest.

Meeks stared at her then shifted nervously in his seat. "I don't have anything to say to you," he told her, his voice full of bitterness and bite.

She pulled the photograph from the files and slid it across the table toward him. "We found this in your apartment. Apparently, you and I were in the same foster home together. Which one is you?"

He stared at the photo then cautiously, as if he wasn't sure about acknowledging it, pointed to a redheaded boy on the end.

She glanced at the picture. "I remember you, Randy. You liked to pick flowers from the yard and give them to Kathryn. She liked them, didn't she?"

He nodded. "She always put them in a glass of water on the windowsill."

Ashlynn nodded. "The house smelled like honeysuckle because of it. That was nice. She was good to you. She wasn't so kind to me."

He lowered his head, obviously aware that her statement was fact.

"How long were you with the Rollinses?"

"Four years. Until she went to jail because of you."

She jumped to defend herself. "She went to jail because of her own actions." Ashlynn bristled and knew she'd misspoken. He'd obviously been happy there and he blamed her for breaking up his family. She had to try another tactic. She pulled the photo of Jacob from the file. "This is my son. He's only four years old. He has nothing to do with any of what happened all those years ago. Please, Randy. Please, if you know anything about him, I just want to bring him home."

He stared at the picture then shook his head. "I don't know anything about your kid and I wasn't involved with any kidnapping. That's all I have to say without my lawyer."

Her heart fell. He'd just shut her down and she knew from experience he was unlikely to offer any information once his lawyer arrived.

She gathered the photos and walked out, aware that she was likely wearing the same expression of disappointment she'd seen on Vince earlier.

Vince sighed then nodded to her. "Don't worry. I'm sure we'll find something inside that van that will get him talking. I'll go put a rush on the lab."

As he walked off, Garrett took her hand. Ashlynn felt a shiver when his fingers closed over hers. His hand was large and strong and she felt so small and comforted by his touch.

"Try not to worry," he said softly. "We found Meeks and we'll find others that will lead us to Jacob."

"I just want him home," she said. She swiped at a tear that slipped from her eye but another followed it and then another so she gave up and let them fall. What did it matter if Garrett saw her crying?

He reached up and wiped away a tear, his finger stroking her cheek tenderly. Once again, she was glad he was here. She needed him by her side. This was one time she didn't have to do it all herself. She had another person she could depend on who understood her need to find Jacob.

She hoped, even dared to pray, she could trust him to stick around this time.

* * *

After the disappointment of being unable to get Meeks to talk, Ashlynn needed to get away from the police station for a while. She asked Garrett to drive her and he agreed. But she hadn't realized how entering her own neighborhood would affect her. They passed her street and Ashlynn felt a pang of sorrow. So much had happened here. Mira had been murdered, Jacob had been stolen from her and she'd been shot at.

Garrett pulled into Olivia's driveway and they got out. Olivia threw her arms around Ashlynn the moment she opened the door, and Ashlynn knew she'd made the right decision in coming here. She needed the encouragement her friend offered. She greeted Garrett, then pulled Ashlynn into the house. She poured them both a cup of coffee, then placed one in front of Ashlynn. "How are you holding up?"

"I can't believe this is really happening. And now this all may have a connection to my past. I feel like my entire life is falling apart." Tears filled her eyes, but she didn't push them back. This was one place she felt comfortable showing her emotions. "I just want him back. I want to hold him and rock him and tell him I love him. I'm so frightened I may never get that chance again."

Olivia glanced at Garrett, who was outside on the patio, standing guard while also giving them some privacy. "I can't believe I finally got to meet the ranger. He's just as hunky as you described. No wonder Stephen didn't measure up."

Ashlynn gasped. "What? That's not true. I did love

Stephen. He was a wonderful husband. He's the one who left. The divorce was his idea, not mine."

"Yes, he was a wonderful husband and a good father. You should have appreciated him more."

Ashlynn frowned. Why was Olivia attacking her?

Olivia set down her coffee cup then sighed. "I'm sorry. I shouldn't have said that. You're already going through so much. You don't need me piling on."

"Do you really believe that about me?"

"Ashlynn, I love you, but nothing is ever good enough for you. You had a great husband, a sweet little boy, a nice home. I don't understand why that was never enough for you." Her voice faltered and Ashlynn realized Olivia was going through something herself. Her friend had lost her husband and her son in a car wreck three years prior, and Ashlynn was certain Jacob's abduction was only bringing up painful memories for her. She'd bonded with Jacob, often offering to babysit or take him for an afternoon at the park.

Ashlynn couldn't help the way her eyes kept being drawn to the photos on the mantel. Olivia's son had been four when he'd died, the same age as Jacob was now, and Ashlynn noticed the two boys shared similar coloring and stature.

Was it possible…?

She pushed that thought away immediately. Olivia was her friend. She would never betray Ashlynn in such a manner. But Ken's words kept floating to her mind. He'd been talking about Bridgette, not Olivia, but she felt they were still applicable. Jealousy was a powerful emotion that often led rational people to do the unthinkable.

Could grief have turned to obsession for her friend?

Ashlynn set her coffee mug on the table. "May I use your bathroom?"

Olivia smiled. "Of course. Go right ahead. I believe I'll go see if your ranger friend would like a cup of coffee."

Ashlynn walked down the hall but glanced back, making sure Olivia was out of sight before she rushed through the house checking each room, throwing open closet doors and even looking behind the shower curtain. She found no sign of Jacob and for that she was relieved, but that didn't mean her friend wasn't involved.

She saw herself in the bathroom mirror and realized she was the one who'd become obsessed. Look what her anxiety had led her to. She was accusing her friend and searching her house. She buried her face in her hands and let the tears come. She wanted this to be over and she wanted Jacob home.

Olivia had been right when she'd said those things. Ashlynn should have been more appreciative of what she'd had. It was a revelation, a wake-up call. She'd been so focused on what she didn't have and how life kept pushing her down that she hadn't stopped to appreciate all she did have. Stephen had tried to tell her as much and she hadn't wanted to listen, but now, too late, she realized the truth.

God had been trying to bless her all along but she hadn't been paying attention.

* * *

As they left Olivia's, Garrett watched Ashlynn gently touch the raw mark around her neck from Meeks's attack. Anger still burned in him over that and he knew Meeks should be thankful Garrett wasn't the kind of man to exact revenge. His heart hammered just remembering the look of terror on Ashlynn's face when he'd entered and seen the knife to her throat.

As it was, Meeks wasn't talking. And a text from Vince delivered more bad news. They hadn't uncovered any evidence in Meeks's apartment that could link him to Jacob's abduction. As of now, only the van and the unknown witness Garrett had spoken to pointed to his involvement. And they hadn't been able to track down the guy Garrett had cornered outside the shop. Garrett suspected he had headed home the moment they'd left and was long gone once the police arrived.

He and Ashlynn had reluctantly returned to the cabin, each hyperaware that forty-eight hours had passed and they were no closer to bringing Jacob home.

He walked over and tossed another log onto the fire in the fireplace as Ashlynn remained curled up on the couch.

"How do you do it?" Ashlynn asked him as he poked the fire.

He glanced up at her. "Do what?"

"How do you have such faith? I confess I've never been much of a religious person, but I envy those that have faith. Everything seems to work out for them."

He looked back at the fire. "God never promised we wouldn't have trouble. He only promised to be with us through it. Even the most faithful have times of trouble." He was thinking of Marcus, who had been one of the most faithful men of God he'd known. It hadn't prevented something bad from happening to him.

Her tone hardened. "Well, He hasn't ever been here for me."

He turned back to look at her and was devastated by the sadness on her face. "He's always been there, Ashlynn. We don't always see Him or feel Him, but He's there."

She folded her arms tighter against her chest and seemed to sink farther into the couch. "I wish I could believe that, but it feels like He doesn't care about me at all. My life has been one terrible thing happening after another. He could have intervened. He could have kept Kathryn Rollins from beating me nearly to death. He could have prevented my mother's death. He didn't do any of that and I would be okay with it if He had only intervened when Jacob was taken." Tears slipped from her eyes. "He's just a little boy. He doesn't deserve to be punished for my faults."

Garrett moved to sit beside her on the couch. "What are you talking about? What faults?"

"I don't know, but it must be something about me or something I've done to make God hate me."

He was horrified that she could actually believe that, but he could see she did.

"God does not hate you, Ashlynn."

"Then why does He keep punishing me?" she asked, her voice choked with emotion.

He quickly pulled her into his arms and hugged

her tightly. She didn't protest, and after a moment she leaned into the crook of his shoulder. He held her while she wept for her son and for all she'd been through.

When her tears were spent, he watched the fire and listened to the steady sound of her breathing as she slipped into sleep. He wished he could do more, say more, to help ease her pain, but he had no answer to why God hadn't intervened. Evil existed in this world. Garrett knew that firsthand. He'd witnessed the evil of men during his time with the rangers. God had not intervened to stop the ambush that had taken the lives of his friends. He'd struggled with that, too, and had never come up with an answer.

But what he did know, what he'd come to count on, was that God had been right there with him during that terrible time and every day since. They surely needed some of that divine intervention right now to find out who was behind the attacks on Ashlynn and where they'd taken Jacob. Once again, his mind drifted to the idea that he was a father and he could imagine a life with Jacob and Ashlynn, as part of a family, but a nagging doubt reminded him that he wasn't cut out to be a father.

He tensed when he heard movement outside.

He slid carefully away from Ashlynn, letting her remain asleep against the arm of the couch as he got up and walked to the back door. He reached for his gun and stepped outside, his ears alert and listening for the rustle. Logic told him it was only a raccoon or a possum, and it probably was, but he needed to be certain.

He heard movement again from the side of the house

and raised his gun. He shone the flashlight into the area and walked in that direction. More rustling sent his senses reeling. Someone was out there in the woods.

Just then, someone jumped from the shadows and tackled him, forcing Garrett to the ground. The man slammed his fist into Garrett's face sending blinding pain soaring through him. But his only thought was of Ashlynn asleep inside. He had to get to her.

He blocked the man's next punch and shoved him hard away, crawling over and smashing his own fists into the intruder's face, then grabbing his gun and hitting him again. The man groaned and immediately collapsed. Garrett knew he'd lost consciousness.

The lack of direct light meant he couldn't get a good look at the man's face, but he could see enough to know he didn't recognize him. He was, however, the right build to be the man who had attacked them at Ashlynn's house, and the automatic rifle he carried further cemented that reasoning. He pulled out his phone and was about to call Vince for backup when another rustle of movement grabbed his attention.

The guy on the ground wasn't alone.

There was someone else in the woods.

Garrett grabbed the automatic rifle, hopped up and hurried back into the house. The cabin was compromised and they had to get out now.

EIGHT

He pulled Ashlynn awake. "They found us," he said, and although her eyes were blurry when she first roused, they immediately cleared. She quickly slipped on her shoes.

Her eyes widened when she saw the rifle he carried. "Where did you get that?"

"I knocked one of them out, but there's at least one other person out there. Possibly more."

He grabbed her hand to leave just as something crashed through the front window, hit the floor and rolled across the floor. Garrett immediately recognized it as a flash bomb. He'd seen his share of them in combat and had used them often in his search-and-rescue missions.

"Get down," he hollered, pulling her behind the couch with him and covering her with his body as the bomb exploded, basking the room in white light and emitting an awful squeal and smoke. The blast sent his senses reeling, as it was meant to do, but he had enough of his wits to pull off his overshirt, rip it in half and hand one piece to Ashlynn. "Cover your mouth and nose." He pressed the fabric to his face and reached for the rifle. They had to get out of here, and fast, before they both passed out from smoke inhalation or the assailant busted into the house and shot them.

The flash bomb had come through the front window, which wasn't good. The car was parked out front and they needed to get to it if they hoped to escape. They would be sitting ducks if they tried to make it out on foot.

He slid the keys into her hand. "I'm going to cover you. I need you to get to the car and start it."

She nodded and started to move toward the door, doing her best to stay low. He followed her, and once they reached it, he dropped the mask and threw open the door.

"Run!" he shouted at her, firing indiscriminately into the woods as Ashlynn ran for the car. He followed her, keeping a steady stream of gunfire going. She started the car and he slid into the passenger seat.

"Go!" he said, once he was inside.

The moment they pulled away, the gunfire started again, coming from the trees to the north. Garrett leaned out the window and shot back, but bullets hit the car and Ashlynn screamed as one shattered the back window. But she didn't let up on the accelerator.

Good girl, he thought. He emptied what remained of the rifle's ammunition into the woods then tossed it and reached for his pistol.

Garrett looked back and saw a man emerge from the brush. He lifted his gun and fired several shots, one of which obviously hit a tire because Garrett heard a loud pop. Ashlynn screamed as the car spun out of control and slid off the road into a ditch.

Garrett took only a moment to recover from the adrenaline pumping through him before kicking open his door and climbing out. He reached inside, hurrying Ashlynn along before the shooter came after them.

"We have to take cover," he said pulling her into the woods, glad she didn't bother pointing out to him that he'd told her they would never make it out alive on foot. The woods were their only choice for safety now.

He glanced back at the cabin. He couldn't see the man anymore, but he would be following them soon. Garrett wanted nothing more than to wait for him, confront him and demand to know why he was targeting Ashlynn and where Jacob was being kept, but right now he had to keep her alive. That had to be his priority. What he wouldn't give for some ranger backup now. He stopped only long enough to slip out his phone and dial Josh's number.

"The cabin was compromised," he said when Josh answered, and his friend responded without hesitation.

"I'm on my way to get you. There's a dirt road about a mile north of the cabin. Stay on that road as long as you can. I'll find you."

Garrett clicked off and slipped the phone into his pocket. Now they only had to stay alive until Josh could get to them.

They ran for what seemed like an hour before they stumbled upon the road Josh mentioned. Garrett was convinced they'd given their attacker the slip. The darkness had been on their side and for that he was thankful.

He heard a car approach and pushed Ashlynn off the road, down behind a clump of bushes. He clutched his gun, ready to use it if needed. He tensed, his whole body on alert at the thought of going into a firefight with only the half-full clip of his pistol. But he wouldn't let them take her. He would do whatever he had to do to protect her.

God, please help me keep her safe.

The vehicle that approached slowed as it neared them. He saw a rapid flash of the headlights in a steady beat and breathed a sigh of relief. That had been their code in the rangers, so he knew it was Josh behind the wheel. He stepped out and flagged down the vehicle. It pulled up beside them and Garrett hurried Ashlynn into the back while he slid into the front seat.

"You made it," Garrett said, so glad to see his friend. "Are you both okay?"

He nodded then looked at Ashlynn.

"I'm not hurt," she said, but he noticed her body was rigid and tired after another close call.

Garrett turned back to Josh. "How did they find us? I can't figure that out. I've disabled the tracking on the car and our cell phones. Only a few people knew where we were." A terrible thought stung him. "There's only one answer. Someone close to us is either passing information to the shooter…or he *is* the shooter."

Ashlynn glanced at him and saw where his line of thinking was headed. "Vince."

He nodded. "Vince."

"You don't really believe Vince is crooked, do you? I've known him for years."

"Did you tell anyone where we were?"

She shook her head. "No, I didn't tell anyone."

"So only Vince knew. That kind of narrows down the pool of suspects, doesn't it?"

She shook her head. "I find it difficult to believe that Vince is in on a plot to murder me and take my son."

"It doesn't necessarily have to be him," Josh said. "He has officers under him that might have access to that information."

Garrett sighed. "Look, I haven't known Vince for that long, but we have to face the facts. Someone is tracking us and we can't trust anyone, not even the police. We'll stay in contact with them for any new leads on Jacob's whereabouts. We'll gather their information, but from this point forward everyone is suspect. We trust no one."

He locked eyes on her to drive home his point. "We're on our own."

Josh pulled into his garage and pushed the button to close the door.

"I should have brought you here in the first place," he said. "I just thought the cabin would be safe."

"I thought so, too," Garrett said. "It should have been."

Josh led them inside. "Ashlynn, you can take the guest bedroom upstairs. Garrett, you can bunk down here on the couch."

Ashlynn went upstairs but her mind wouldn't stop

running. Garrett suspected someone close to them was behind the attacks on her and she was beginning to believe him. But now she was on edge. She didn't know who to trust. The only person she was certain she could rely upon was Garrett, which was a strange and new sensation.

She still had a difficult time believing Vince was behind the attacks on her, but Garrett was right. They had to be careful. However, she realized there was another person besides Vince who had known they were at the cabin.

She got up and quietly opened the bedroom door and peeked out. The house was dark and quiet, and she was glad. She needed to speak with Garrett without Josh around. She padded downstairs and found him stretched out on the couch. He wasn't asleep and jumped up when he saw her. "Hey, what's up?" he asked, his face taking on a worried expression. "Is everything okay?"

She sat beside him on the couch, uncertain how to voice her suspicion. "I know you said we couldn't trust anyone. What about Josh? Is it possible—?"

"Don't even go there," he said, stopping her before she finished her question. "I trust him. In fact, there's no one I trust more than Josh and the rangers. He's on our side."

"I can appreciate you have a connection with him, but that doesn't mean—"

"Ash, I trust Josh. Period. You have no idea what we've been through together. He would never betray me."

"I'm sure you believe that, but it's just that this is

Jacob we're talking about. This is our son, Garrett. We have to think about his safety. How can we truly trust anyone?"

"If I can't trust the rangers, then who can I trust? I can't continue to live my life on the defensive, constantly wondering who is on my side and who is going to let me down. That's an exhausting way to exist."

She clenched her jaw, taking his comment as a direct hit at her. "Sometimes it's a necessity, especially when everyone around you continually lets you down."

He nodded then stood. "Okay, I deserved that."

"No, I'm not only talking about you, Garrett. Stephen, too. My foster mother. My friends. I couldn't even trust my own father to be there for me. Why does everyone I know let me down? Am I that terrible a person?"

He pulled her into his arms as her chin quivered. "No, baby. You're not a terrible person. You're an incredibly amazing, determined, powerful woman."

"Then why does everyone leave me?" Even she could hear the pitiful desperation in her voice but she couldn't stop it. It was a question she'd pondered for years. What was so bad about her that no one wanted her?

He must have seen her desperation because he grabbed her arms, sending a spark of electricity between them. "It's not because of you, Ashlynn. I didn't leave because of you. It was me. I was afraid of letting you down. I knew I could never live up to the memories of the men who died the night our team was ambushed."

She was surprised by the intensity of the pain she saw on his face when he spoke about the ambush. She'd held back pressing him about the events of that night mostly because she hadn't wanted him to use it as an excuse for his actions. But now…well, she wanted to know.

"What happened on that mountain?" she asked him, her voice soft and encouraging. "And why did it have to take you away from me?"

He gulped and pulled back from her. She saw the flash of horror and pain that spread across his face and knew he was reluctant to relive that night. She wondered again if maybe she shouldn't press him, but pushed that concern away. She'd loved him so much. She deserved to know what terrible thing had taken him from her.

His folded his arms across his chest. His stance was stiff and his jaw set. She saw how painful it was for him to relive that night and felt guilty for even asking. She had no right to demand this of him. She jumped up and stood behind him, wrapping her arms around him and resting her head against his shoulder. She could feel him shaking and knew at that moment that she wouldn't press him for details. "Never mind. You don't have to tell me."

He blew out a deep, fortifying breath. "It's time you know the truth and I suppose it's time I talked about it. I've never spoken to anyone about what happened, not even to Josh or the other rangers. There was never any reason. They were there. They knew what occurred."

He stepped away from her, unable or unwilling to look at her as he told the story. She didn't press that. Instead, she gave him the space he needed. She sat on the couch, holding her breath in anticipation of what he was about to share and lifting a silent prayer for his pain. It seemed so great.

"I was the first one in," he said, his voice cracking. He stopped to clear his throat and started again. "I was on point. My friend Marcus was following behind me and the rest of the squad was scattered out, taking different positions. Our target was a high-profile Taliban leader who'd been hiding out in the mountains and we'd finally gotten some good intel on his whereabouts. Command brought in some Delta operators along with some SEALs to lead the mission. Our part was to go in with them. They would go after the target while we cleared the compound.

"I saw Levi approach a tent. Three women emerged, all strapped with explosives. I screamed for him to watch out, but they went off right before my eyes. Levi went flying."

He shook his head in amazement. "I still don't know how he ever survived that explosion. Then shots rang out. They seemed to come from everywhere. Marcus was standing beside me and the next thing I knew he just convulsed and hit the ground. Blood was everywhere. I leaned down to help him and then it was all over me, too. I knew I had to get him out of there but everyone was shooting and shouting and screaming."

His voice cracked again, but he continued. "Smoke

was thick as the night and the air stank of gunpowder and fuel. I grabbed Marcus and tried to drag him toward a building, trying to find some pocket of peace so I could check his wounds, but the shots just kept coming. The whole time Marcus was begging me to take care of his family."

She gasped at the horror of what he'd been through. But he wasn't done.

"I knew I had to get him back to where he could get some medical help. And I just panicked. I picked up my weapon and started shooting. When my gun was empty, I picked up his." He leaned his head into his hands. "I killed a lot of people that night, all in the name of war."

She shook her head and instinctively moved to him, placing her hand reassuringly on his back. "No, you were trying to survive and you were trying to help your friend."

"I pulled him up over my shoulder and carried him out. I tried to get him back to the truck." Garrett's shoulders shook. "I knew it was a lost cause. I knew he was gone, but I couldn't leave him. But then I saw Levi. I heard his moan and I saw his leg move. He was alive. I could hardly believe it. At first I thought my eyes were playing tricks on me, but he was moving. He was alive and Marcus was dead. There was no way I could carry them both out of there so I left Marcus and went after Levi. The search-and-rescue teams tried to go in after the firefight and retrieve the bodies of those who'd died…fourteen men in all…but they didn't find his body. They never did recover it. His family had nothing to bury. And when I think about all the terrible things that probably happened to his body, I shudder because I've seen the evil that lives over there and because I left him to suffer it."

"You did the right thing," she told him. "You saved Levi. You said yourself that Marcus was gone. You couldn't have saved him. What about Levi? Did he survive?"

He nodded. "He was hurt badly, probably worse than any of the rest of us that lived. And he doesn't remember a lot of what happened. Sometimes I think he's the fortunate one, not to have a memory of that terrible night."

Her heart broke at Garrett's story. He had indeed been through an ordeal and she understood how such an event could have affected him. She only wished he'd been able to talk to her about it then. Things would have been so different if she'd only known.

"I never knew anything about the ambush," she said. "No one contacted me about it and I didn't hear it on the news."

"They wouldn't have contacted you," he told her. "I hadn't had the opportunity to update my emergency information. And I didn't have a next of kin so the army didn't call anyone on my behalf. As for the news, I'm sure the government buried that story along with all the soldiers that died on that mountain. It was a failed attempt to take down a powerful enemy." The bite in his tone was real and bitter. "They wouldn't want such details broadcast."

But something he'd said touched a nerve with her. The army had had no one to contact on Garrett's behalf. It saddened her that he'd been so alone. And he'd remained alone. She had to remind herself that it was by choice. He'd had a family. He just hadn't known it.

"I stayed with the rangers for a while after that, but then I just couldn't continue. Every time I went into a firefight, I found myself reliving that night and hating myself for leaving Marcus behind. The doctors called it survivor's guilt and it nearly killed me. I was alone for a long while. I spent my time after the rangers doing things—risky things—that more than once should have killed me. I truly don't know how I'm still alive except by the grace of God. Anyway, after a while, I realized that I didn't want to be alone anymore so Josh found me this job and I came back to Jackson. I still don't know why God kept me alive that night, but I'm glad He did, Ashlynn, because now I get to be the one here for you and Jacob."

At the same time she was realizing how sad she felt for Garrett, she also realized she was in a similar situation. She'd spent her life alone, protecting her heart from getting hurt again. But it hadn't worked because she was hurting now and it wasn't because her son had rejected her. It was because opening her heart to Jacob had also meant opening it up to pain.

But she wouldn't have changed it. She couldn't stop loving Jacob any more than she could stop breathing. Having him had made her life so much richer. Nothing, not even losing him now, could take away the joy and happiness he'd brought to her life.

But that was also true for her time with Garrett. She'd held back for years, trying to protect herself from the pain he'd caused when he'd broken their engagement. But she wouldn't give up the memories of their time together, would she? Aside from giving her Jacob, Garrett had shown her what real love looked like and for the first time in her life had given her some reason to keep going after all the terrible things that had happened to her.

She hugged him tightly and he clung to her. She finally understood the circumstances that had separated them. It still hurt, but now her heart broke for him more than just for herself. She only wished he'd been able to turn to her during that awful time, that she'd been able to be there for him as a wife would have been, but she'd never been given that opportunity.

Her heart cried out for all the pain and sadness they'd both endured. *Oh, God, please help mend our shattered lives.*

The next morning, Garrett stood in Josh's kitchen and watched the morning news on TV as they replayed Ashlynn's emotional plea for Jacob's return. His mind ran over the evidence they had, which wasn't much, and knew they had to be missing something. They were still no closer to finding his son and that distressed him. He'd made a promise that he would bring Jacob home and he meant more than ever to keep it.

Speaking to her last night, sharing the details of the ambush, had been like having a weight lifted from his shoulders. Although he didn't like the way he'd lost control of his emotions and hadn't wanted her to see how weak he really was, hearing her assurances that he hadn't done anything wrong had been like a balm soothing his rugged heart and smoothing out some of the rough patches inside of him. He was thankful for that opportunity and knew he'd been right to come back to Jackson. Josh had been correct in his assertion that Garrett needed to reconnect to life and people. He'd been alone for far too long.

Ashlynn came downstairs and joined him at the kitchen table. She looked beautiful. Her eyes were still blurry from sleep, but he could tell she'd gotten some rest. He used the remote to click off the TV then poured her a cup of coffee and handed it to her as he placed a gentle kiss on her forehead. "How did you sleep?"

She gave him a small but weary smile and sipped her coffee. "As well as I could." She motioned towards the television. "Any update?"

"No. I called Vince earlier, too, and none of the tips that have come in have led anywhere. But if he's involved, he'll want to bury any that might lead back to him."

She nodded but her heart seemed so heavy. She set her phone on the counter. "I've been trying to keep up, too, but the news apps don't have any more information, either."

"Don't you give up, Ashlynn. We're going to find him and bring him home. This isn't over."

She nodded but her agreement didn't reach her eyes.

"I know the statistics, Garrett. Children that aren't re-covered in the first forty-eight hours are unlikely to be found." Her voice caught as she continued. "It's al-ready been over sixty hours since he was abducted."

He knelt beside her and rubbed her face. "I don't listen to statistics. I'm not giving up on our son…or on you." He leaned forward to place another kiss on her forehead, but she stopped him, placing a gentle one on his lips, instead. His heart hammered at the soft-ness of her mouth and the taste of salt still lingering, most likely from a tear-filled night. He waited for her to make excuses for her action or pull away, but when she didn't, he pulled her to him for a long, deep kiss that was new and familiar all at once.

It ended when her phone rang, interrupting the mo-ment.

She glanced at the screen. "That's Ken. I should answer it."

He nodded and stepped away from her. She picked up the phone and spoke a few words before turning to Garrett. "Hang on, Ken. I'm going to put you on speaker so Garrett can hear this, too." She placed the phone back on the counter and hit the speaker button. "Go ahead."

"I was telling Ashlynn that I did some more dig-ging into Randy Meeks's background. After he was removed from the Rollins home, he bounced around from foster home to foster home before aging out of the program. He's been in and out of trouble with the law for most of his juvenile and adult life."

Garrett nodded. "We already know all of this from his police record."

"Oh, well, did you know Kathryn Rollins, your foster mother, Ashlynn, was being investigated as part of a baby-selling ring? Some have even speculated that someone connected to the ring murdered her to shut her up because she had agreed to speak with the FBI in exchange for a reduced sentence on the abuse charges."

Ashlynn gasped. "Baby selling? I had no idea."

"You wouldn't have. You were just a child then, and the FBI took notice of her only after she was imprisoned."

Garrett looked at her. "It's possible someone from the ring took Jacob."

She shook her head. "That was so long ago. Why would they wait until now to target me? If they wanted to hurt me, they could have snatched Jacob when he was a baby. Why wait until now?"

Ken had the answer. "The perpetrator could have been in jail all this time and only recently got out. Or he could have inadvertently reconnected with you recently and it re-sparked his anger towards you. Kathryn made them a lot of money and someone could be harboring anger at you for costing them that money."

"It's seems so implausible."

"It's a lead, Ashlynn, and unless you have some other news I'm not aware of, it's the best one we have."

Garrett thought the other man's tone sounded harsh, but Ashlynn didn't seem to react to it. He supposed Ken was just as weary and worried as the rest of them. "You should go through your case files again, this time looking for any name that might spark recognition. Anyone from your past could be suspect."

She nodded. "I don't remember running into anyone from my past recently. I think I would know them."

"You didn't recognize Meeks," Ken reminded her and she blushed at his assertion. She couldn't deny it.

Reluctantly, she agreed to give her case files another look.

Ken continued. "I've contacted the FBI agent in charge of the investigation back then. He's agreed to meet with us and discuss the possibility that Jacob's kidnapping is related to someone involved in the baby-selling ring. I told him to meet us at your office in an hour."

Ashlynn looked at Garrett as if for confirmation. "I'm not sure how I feel about going back to that office after what happened there."

"It's a good lead, Ashlynn, and we need to talk with this guy. He may be the key to locating your son."

Garrett understood her concern, but also knew she would go. She would do whatever it took to get her son back.

"Don't worry," he said. "I'll be right there with you."

"Fine," she told Ken. "We'll meet you there."

He'd been trying so hard not to let Ashlynn get to him, but she had. He hadn't been able to stop her from sneaking back into his heart. Had she ever truly left? He'd been searching for years since the ambush, looking for something to bring meaning to his life but the truth was he'd had it all along. He'd just been too stubborn to realize it.

He steeled his determination and took a deep breath. He wouldn't let them down again. And once they brought Jacob home safely, maybe they could talk about becoming the family they always should have been.

NINE

The downtown streets looked eerily different from their weekday hustle and bustle as Garrett drove them to the DA's offices, but it gave Ashlynn the opportunity to really notice the Christmas decorations on the storefronts for the first time. Her heart saddened thinking about Jacob and wondering if he would be home in time for Christmas.

Bring him home, Lord, she prayed silently not even finding it odd that she'd started seeking God's assistance. If finding her son meant believing in a God that would continually let her down, she would do it. Garrett had told her that God rarely intervened in sin, but that He was always there providing comfort and guidance. She wanted His intervention so much, but she would also gladly take His direction. Other than the kidnappers, no one else knew the location of her son but God so she would place her faith in Him to lead their way. Garrett had assured her that God didn't hate her and all she could do was to hope and pray he was right and her very presence wouldn't cause Him to work against her. Jacob deserved better than that.

All the street parking spaces in front of the office were empty, so Garrett parked in one close to the building. He pulled out the box of files and carried them upstairs. She felt fortunate they hadn't been ruined after their getaway from the cabin, but Garrett had returned with Josh to retrieve his truck and their belongings, and had seen no further signs of the shooters.

She used her key to unlock the suite doors, then pushed them open to allow him inside. Just like with the rest of the building, she heard nothing coming from any of the offices, but Garrett checked them all just to be certain they were alone. They couldn't be too careful after what happened the last time she was here. Many of the associates often worked on Saturdays, but it was well past lunchtime and they had likely headed home by now. As she'd expected, Garrett returned with news that the suite was empty except for them.

She led the way into the conference room, deciding the table there would be more beneficial for the interview with the FBI agent.

Garrett placed the box with her files on the table and Ashlynn pulled out a handful of folders. She wanted to look through them again while they waited for Ken and the agent to arrive. He followed suit, grabbing one and opening it as he sat beside her. "I'm not sure what I'm even looking for," he admitted.

She sighed. "Aside from finding Randy Meeks's name in here, neither do I. But Ken thought it was a good idea."

"Where is he?" Garrett asked. "He was the one who

was so adamant about being here." He glanced at his phone. "They should be here by now."

She shrugged. "I suppose he got caught up with something. He'll be here soon." She pulled open a file and started to read through it, but the sheer volume of names she was now wading through overwhelmed her. "It feels like we're searching for a needle in a haystack and we don't even know which haystack to search in."

"We're following up all the leads. We have to consider this could be connected to one of your cases. This guy knows you, Ashlynn. He's fixated on you. He has a personal connection to you. We have to think you've come across him at some point."

She sighed. "I know. I just don't understand why someone would be targeting me or why they would take Jacob. That's beyond cruel."

And she hadn't been too thrilled with Ken's attitude on the phone, either. She'd glanced at Garrett to see if he'd noticed, but he hadn't seemed fazed by it. Was she being overly emotional? Had the strain of Jacob's abduction and some maniac trying to kill her finally gotten to her? She knew Ken cared about finding Jacob. He'd been working countless hours in addition to his duties at the DA's office to help them.

And she did have to concede his point. She hadn't recognized Meeks. That had been such a long time ago and she had worked so hard to put that life behind her. Judge Warren had told her again and again to stay laser focused on her future and never let her past define her. It was possible she'd run into someone she'd once known and just didn't realize it. Her life was incredibly hectic these days between being a mother, fighting for custody of her child and pursuing a high-pressure career as a prosecutor. But had she been so busy building a future for them that she'd allowed a snake from her past to slither back into their lives?

But digging through her past had brought up some painful memories that had nothing to do with finding Jacob and everything to do with her history with Garrett. Her face warmed as she remembered how she'd kissed him that morning and the incredible kiss he'd returned. Was it possible they could finally have a future together and be that family she'd always dreamed of? She glanced at him and her heart quickened at the idea. Had he grown into a man she and her son could finally rely upon?

She opened another file and skimmed through it, a car hijacking case. She remembered it well. The defendant had carjacked a college-aged girl, and robbed and terrorized her before she'd finally managed to escape. She'd been extremely traumatized and Ashlynn had hoped to give her some relief by putting the repeat offender in prison for a long time.

The case was especially memorable to her because it had come at the same time that Jacob had leaped from the couch and broken his collarbone. She'd been prepping for the trial when she'd gotten the call and had to leave work. She'd also missed a number of days of work caring for him and been forced to push the trial back several weeks.

It hadn't bothered her much back then. That was before they'd hired Mira, and Stephen had been out of town on business and unable to help her, but now it seemed to bring to light every reason she'd had for being angry that Garrett hadn't been around. He'd missed the broken collarbone. He'd missed Jacob's first steps and his first words. He'd missed doctors' appointments and tantrums and even a minor surgery to place tubes in Jacob's ears.

Those darker memories began to flow back to her, every moment when she and Jacob had needed him and he hadn't been there for them. She couldn't forget that. And how could she ever trust that he wouldn't do it again?

She pushed away the files and stood up, trying to stretch the knots out of her stiff muscles.

"You okay?" he asked, coming to stand behind her and wrapping his arms around her.

But she wasn't. The turmoil of not knowing if she could depend on him was just too much for her to keep continually turning over in her mind. It boiled down to one, undeniable truth—she didn't trust him.

"I've tried so hard to put my past behind me and now it seems the key to finding Jacob might lie in my past."

"I know it's hard, but it's necessary."

"It's not just hard, Garrett. It's unbearable. Why do I have to keep reliving it? Why can't these people just leave me alone? Everything in my past keeps coming back to haunt me. Even you, showing up here, dredging up painful memories."

He grimaced at her words and she sighed. She hadn't

really meant to be so cruel. "I'm sorry. I shouldn't have said that."

"It wasn't my intention to hurt you, Ashlynn."

"No, it wasn't your intention, but intentions don't matter, Garrett. You did hurt me. I don't ever want to feel that way again. I realize this isn't really your fault, but I can't get past the feeling that if you'd been here, if you hadn't left us all those years ago, this wouldn't be happening. Jacob would be here with me and he wouldn't have been abducted. I know I shouldn't blame you, but I do. I've tried to get past it. I can't forget how you left us."

She pushed away from Garrett, but he tightened his arms around her. "Don't, Ash. Please, don't push me away."

"I can't do this, Garrett. I just can't."

He touched her face, stroking her cheek with his finger. "I can't pretend I don't care for you. I want you and Jacob to be a part of my life, Ashlynn. I love you. I love you both. I want us to be a family."

Her heart was divided. On one hand, she longed to fall into his embrace and lose herself. He was offering her everything she'd ever dreamed of, a life she'd yearned for all those years ago. But the other side of her heart, the side that had been battered and broken too many times, cried foul. He'd shattered those dreams of happily-ever-after and she'd worked too hard to build a life for herself and Jacob to put it at risk again, especially for someone who had already proven himself unreliable in sticking around when things got tough.

She shook her head, tears springing to her eyes.

She couldn't risk Jacob's future that way. "I can't," she said, her voice choked. She turned away from him. "I can't. This will never work, Garrett. I don't trust you anymore. I don't know how I can ever trust you. How do I know you'll be there for us?"

"I will be."

"I wish I could believe that but I… I just don't."

He sighed and dug his hands into his pockets then put some distance between them. The pain on his face was evident and sharp. She knew she'd hurt him and wanted to insist that that wasn't her intention, but then she smiled, realizing those were the same words he'd expressed to her. Neither of them meant to hurt the other, yet somehow they'd both been hurt.

"I appreciate your help in finding Jacob. I don't know what I would have done if you weren't here, Garrett, but I can't do anything else. Whatever it was we had all those years ago, it ended the day I received your call."

He nodded but didn't speak for several moments. Ashlynn turned away. There was nothing else to say. She'd made her decision and nothing could change that.

His voice was low and gruff with emotion when he spoke. "I think I'll step out and call Josh. See if he's heard anything on those background checks I asked him to do."

She nodded then turned in time to see him walk out of the conference room. She knew she was doing the right thing for herself and her son. She just wished it didn't hurt so badly.

* * *

Once he was clear of the suite, Garrett leaned against the closed door and took a long, steadying breath. Her words had stabbed him, not because they were mean but because they were true. She didn't trust him enough to allow him to be part of her life and her family. He'd lost his opportunity for a family when he'd let them down. It only cemented what he already knew. He wasn't cut out to be a father. He'd tried so hard to pretend he could do it, that he could re-create what they'd lost, but Ashlynn was right. He was a failure.

And he couldn't ask her and Jacob to take on that kind of risk. He should never have returned to town, and some part of him admitted that he had always hoped to run into Ashlynn. He hadn't sought her out, but he couldn't deny he was glad he'd seen her again.

He rubbed his face and looked up at the midday sky. It was a bright blue with little cloud cover and he stared up at it feeling better in such close proximity to his Lord. He didn't understand why God had left him here and he hoped his son and Ashlynn wouldn't suffer because He had.

Please, Father, help me to find Jacob. Don't let my son pay the price for my selfishness. And no matter how Ashlynn feels about me, keep her safe. Father, give me guidance. Light my path.

Even if he couldn't be a part of his family, he would still do everything he could for them before he let them go.

Ashlynn pulled the papers back toward her and tried to concentrate on examining them instead of the wounded look she'd seen on Garrett's face. She couldn't think about that now. She felt terrible about laying this all on him, but after that kiss this morning, she hadn't wanted to lead him on, allow him to believe there was a future for them when there really wasn't. Finding Jacob still had to be her first priority.

She glanced at the clock on the wall, noting he'd been gone for over ten minutes. That made her uncomfortable. The last time he'd let her out of his sight, Meeks had attacked her. She reminded herself that she was in no danger. The suite was empty and Garrett hadn't gone far. He was just giving her space to work. She closed one file and placed it on the readthrough stack before getting another and opening it. She needed something else to concentrate on and hopefully he would return soon enough.

As she flipped through her papers, she landed on a case of domestic abuse from back in the spring. It didn't seem to have any bearing on anything and she nearly added it to the not-relevant pile until she spotted a name she did recognize—Paul Rollins. His name was listed on the defense's list of character witnesses.

She hadn't seen it previously because the case had never gone to trial. The defendant had accepted a plea for a lesser sentence. But she knew the name instantly—Paul Rollins, Kathryn Rollins's biological son. She and Meeks had been fostered in the same home where this man had also lived. He'd been a teenager in the photo they'd recovered from Meeks's apartment. She had no idea what had happened to him after his mother went to prison, but it seemed too coincidental to dismiss that his name had been in her case files. Had he come to court to support his friend during the preliminary phase and seen her there, re-sparking some anger against her, just as Garrett had suggested?

She decided to check him out, just in case. Using her laptop, she typed his name into the police database the DA's office had access to. He had an extensive criminal record. He wouldn't have made much of a character witness in her opinion. She would have torn him apart in court. But when the mug shot of Paul Rollins materialized, she gasped, recognizing the sharp eyes and features she knew so well.

Paul Rollins had been right here in her office many times, getting close to her and probably planning his revenge against her for months.

Fear pulsed through her. She reached for her phone and quickly dialed Garrett's number. He needed to know what she'd found. His phone rang once then went straight to voice mail. Now he wasn't even taking her calls? She waited impatiently for the beep. "Garrett, call me. It's important. I know who's behind the attempts on my life and Jacob's kidnapping. It's Ken."

She hung up the phone, then stood. If Garrett wouldn't accept her calls she would just have to track him down and make him listen to her. She was certain he wouldn't have gone far. He had to still be in the building somewhere or possibly outside. She walked to the window and gazed out, hoping to spot him on the front lawn. She didn't see him, but she instinctively knew he was close.

Suddenly, she heard the main suite door open and

close. Was it Garrett returning? She prayed it was. She headed toward the door but stopped, frozen when she saw it wasn't him.

Ken was approaching the conference room.

Her heart raced and anger bit through her, but she wasn't sure what to do. She wanted to confront him, to demand to know why he'd deceived her and to ask if he took Jacob. But if Ken was truly behind this, she had to be smart. Jacob's life depended on it. Would he attack her once he saw Garrett wasn't around? Or would he continue to play the role of the concerned friend? That thought sickened her.

Oh, God, what do I do?

She grabbed her phone and tried Garrett's number again. It again went straight to voicemail so she shot off a text to him instead.

God, tell him to come back. I need him!

Still uncertain how to react, she turned to face Ken. But his gaze was focused on something behind her. She turned to look and saw her computer screen displaying the image of his mug shot along with his real name. His deception was now out in the open.

His eyes moved to her and his mouth twitched into a self-satisfied grin. "So, you've uncovered my true identity, have you?"

Anger pulsed through her. This man had pretended to be her friend when all along he'd been playing her for a fool. And since they were no longer pretending, she decided confronting him was her only option. "I know who you really are, *Paul*. Where is my son? Where is Jacob?"

"You'll soon find out everything." He took a step in her direction and she instinctively backed away. He grinned, obviously satisfied at the fear his movement had caused in her. She had to get away from him, to find Garrett and end this once and for all. This man was responsible for all the heartache and pain in her life recently. He'd killed Stephen and Mira, and tried to kill her, too. And she'd led him right to herself each time, believing him a friend and confidant. He'd always known their location and had used that to his advantage in planning his revenge.

"You were the one who drugged me," she said. "It wasn't Judge Warren's brownies at all."

"No, it wasn't. I took an opportunity to distract Bridgette and slipped it into your coffee." He removed a syringe from his pocket. "In fact, I was able to get my hands on another dose. My girlfriend, Barbara, is an LPN over at the medical center. At least, she was until she agreed to run away with me and my son."

Ashlynn gasped. "*Your* son? Jacob is not your son."

"That doesn't matter to her. I've got her convinced we're protecting Jacob from you. She's a pushover for a nice smile and a sad story."

He moved again and Ashlynn did, too. She couldn't allow him to drug her again. She took off, running around the table, but the room wasn't large and he was able to reach out and grab her, taking hold of her arm and pulling her toward him. She kicked and struggled but was no match for his strength. He wrapped his arm around her neck, blocking her airway, then injected the syringe into her neck. She kicked and flailed, sending papers from the table flying, but she couldn't land a shot that loosened his tight hold on her and she couldn't breathe in enough air to even moan much less scream for help.

Finally, she went limp in his arms and felt herself fading, unable to stop it. She only had two hopes now—Garrett and God. She silently prayed for God's intervention. *Don't let me die without knowing Jacob's safe*, her heart cried.

He lowered her to the floor and stood over her. As she finally faded into unconsciousness, he whispered something in her ear that haunted her soul.

"I warned you there were a lot of crazies out there."

"Don't give up hope," Josh said when Garrett phoned him and finally spilled everything—his nervousness about being a father, his rekindled feelings for Ashlynn and even her insistence that she could never trust him. "Trust is earned. You'll just have to prove it to her. I know you have it in you to be a great husband and father," Josh insisted. "Just remember, God is the Great Restorer."

Garrett took a deep, cleansing breath. "Thanks, Josh. I needed to hear that." He could always count on his friends be to there to lift him up when he was down. One more reason reconnecting with people had been the right decision for him.

"I know you're still struggling, but don't give up believing that God is on your side, Garrett. He left you here—He left us all here—for a reason. Right now your family needs you. That's your reason."

He realized Josh was right. His family needed him and he would be here for them. He would find Jacob and he would bring him home to his mother. He owed them both that and he needed to concentrate on that instead of on his own aching shell of a heart.

He was a ranger and it was time he started acting like it.

"Have you found anything in those background checks I asked you to do?" Garrett directed the focus of the conversation back to the finding of Jacob.

Josh didn't flinch at his abrupt change of gear. "No red flags on any of the names you gave me."

He sighed, unsure if he was glad Ashlynn had no friends who were betraying her or upset that they still had no leads.

"Thanks. I'll call you later." He hung up with Josh and walked back upstairs to the suite. He pushed open the door and immediately saw the conference room was empty. Case files were scattered on the floor, which made his heart quicken with apprehension.

"Ashlynn," he called, hoping against hope that she'd taken a bathroom break or gone to the supply closet. But he knew better. A thousand scenarios rushed through his mind. Maybe she'd thought he wasn't coming back. Would she have left without him? And where would she have gone?

He pulled out his phone and saw two missed calls from her. He kicked himself. She must have phoned while he was on the call with Josh. Why hadn't he noticed? He saw she'd left him a voicemail.

"Garrett, call me. It's important. I know who's behind the attempts on my life and Jacob's kidnapping. It's Ken."

He held his breath. She'd figured out Ken was behind this? And now she was gone. Had she gone after Ken when Garrett didn't answer? Or had he shown up and grabbed her? How had he not seen Ken enter the building? He tried her phone and heard it ring. He followed the sound and found it on the floor beneath the table.

Not good.

He dialed Ken's phone and it went straight to voicemail. That didn't really answer his question. He was the one who'd convinced them to come to the office then hadn't shown up. Had he lured them there? Or had Ashlynn gotten out before he'd arrived?

He pulled his gun and hurried out, searching the hall, the stairwell and the outer offices. If Ken had grabbed her, he couldn't have gotten far pulling someone with him. He worked his way down through the building but found no sign of Ashlynn or Ken. As he pulled open the double glass doors that led outside, fear and regret soared through him.

And that old nagging guilt returned to him. He'd let her down again.

Garrett kicked open the door of Ken's apartment and burst inside, gun drawn and ready for a fight. Josh, Vince and several officers followed him. The apartment was empty. He hadn't really expected to find them here, but it was the only place he knew to start looking. The others fanned out and checked the rest of the apartment.

"It's clear," Vince said, after checking the back rooms. "They're not here."

Garrett felt frustration wash over him. Security cameras at the DA's offices had confirmed that Ken had, indeed, abducted Ashlynn. It had shown him carrying her to his car. Garrett had taken her case files from the office, hoping to find something in them that would lead him to answers, but so far they'd found nothing. They needed to learn everything they could about Ken Barrett and quick. Why had he taken Ashlynn? Why had he kidnapped Jacob? And was he behind the deaths of Stephen and Mira? Everything seemed to point to the fact that Ken had a grudge against Ashlynn, only they still didn't know why.

He scanned the apartment. It was sparsely furnished and held no visible personal effects. In the kitchen he found a photo taped to the refrigerator. It looked like the same photo Meeks had had in his apartment. Only in this picture, a red circle had been drawn around Ashlynn's face and a big red X marked through it.

Had Ken gotten a copy of the image from Meeks? Or did he have some connection to the foster home where Ashlynn had grown up? He was frustrated by all the questions that still remained unanswered.

Vince approached him. "I've got a BOLO out for Ken's car and a trace on his phone. He must have turned it off because it's not pinging anywhere."

Garrett nodded. "He's smart and he knows police procedures." He shook his head. "There must be something we're missing." He turned to Josh. "You did those background checks on Ken. Did you find anything that seemed suspicious?"

Josh took out his phone and pulled up a file. "Nothing that raised any red flags. He's worked as an investigator with the DA's office for six months. Before that, he worked as a parole officer in Pennsylvania for twenty-six years until he moved to be closer to his daughter and her family. Exemplary performance records."

"Wait, you said he moved here to be closer to his daughter?"

"That's what his supervisors at Philly PD told me on the phone. Why?"

His gut started screaming that something wasn't adding up. "Because Ken told me he didn't have any children."

Josh pulled up the file on Ken again and Garrett watched over his shoulder as an official photograph appeared. His heart sank. "Is this from the file Philly PD sent over?"

Josh nodded. "What's wrong?"

Garrett felt a rush of dread pulse through him. The man in the photograph was gray haired and round, not sharp featured and thin. It wasn't that he just looked different. He was someone else completely. "That isn't Ken Barrett. I've never seen that man before."

Their Ken was an imposter and now they had no idea who the man they were searching for really was.

Garrett paced in front of Vince's desk as Vince spoke with the commander of the precinct in Philadelphia where Ken had supposedly worked for twenty-six years. His face was pale when he hung up and Garrett knew his worst suspicions were confirmed.

Vince checked the computer. "The prints the DA's office has on file for Ken are faked, but we lifted prints from the conference room. We recovered a set that wasn't on file so we ran them through other databases including the military database and got a hit." He pulled up Ken's photo on the big screen. "His real name is Paul Rollins, a former army sniper."

Garrett's heart sank. He glanced at Josh and knew his friend was thinking the same thing he was. A former army sniper would be well versed in weaponry and extremely dangerous. He scanned through Rollins's file. "His mother's name was Kathryn Rollins." He looked at them. "That was Ashlynn's foster mother, the woman that nearly killed her when she was young. Her testimony helped send Kathryn to prison where she was murdered."

"So this is all about revenge," Josh said. "He's getting back at her because she had his mother sent to prison."

Garrett's blood boiled at the realization. His family was in danger all because someone wanted revenge on a girl who'd been beaten and tortured. But he had to keep his calm if he hoped to bring her and Jacob home safely.

"I'm going to call him," Garrett said, pulling out his phone. "He wiped the computer clean and made sure I didn't see him at the office, so he may assume we don't know he's the one behind all this. I'll call him to see if he's heard anything and we'll try to get a trace on his phone."

"You tried earlier and it went straight to voicemail. He's probably got it turned off," Josh stated.

Garrett shrugged. "I have to keep trying. What do I have to lose?"

Vince nodded. "I'll set up the trace."

A few minutes later, Garrett placed the call. It sickened him to speak to Ken like nothing was wrong, but he knew he had to hold his tongue if they hoped to track him.

Ken answered on the third ring. "Garrett, I heard about Ashlynn. Any news?" he asked, his voice kind and full of concern.

"No," Garrett told him. "Have you heard anything?"

"I'm afraid all I've hit are dead ends," Ken said. "I'll keep searching, but so far I've turned up nothing that could help us find her."

Vince gave him a thumbs-up, indicating that they were able to track Ken's cell phone. Garrett noted it was downtown. "Well, keep me informed," he said. But then he couldn't stop himself from issuing a warning. "If anything happens to her, I won't stop until whoever is responsible pays." He hoped the warning rang through. He didn't want Ken to know they were on to him, but he also wanted him to be on alert that Garrett was coming for whoever had taken Ashlynn.

Ken was silent for a moment and Garrett wondered if he'd hung up. Then he said sympathetically, "You really love her, don't you?"

He couldn't stop the emotion that crept into his

voice. "Very much. And I won't stop until I find her. That's a promise."

Ken clicked off and Garrett instinctively knew he'd shown his hand. But Vince was already barking orders to mobilize the task force.

"We're headed downtown to the old Royal Hotel," he said. "It's been abandoned for years but there are always squatters. He must be holed up there." Vince patted his back. "Don't worry. We'll get him."

Garrett knew it would take Vince time to organize the task force…time Ashlynn and Jacob might not have. He glanced at Josh, who nodded, obviously understanding that, too. He motioned to Garrett to follow him then went outside to his car and opened the trunk. It was loaded down with enough weapons and gear to equip a small army.

"I'll phone Levi on the way and tell him to meet us there."

Josh slammed the trunk closed and they both got into his car.

He had no doubt he was going to get Ken. His days of freedom were now limited. Garrett only hoped Ken hadn't yet harmed Ashlynn or Jacob.

A heavy weight pressed on her head as Ashlynn regained consciousness. She struggled to remember what had happened to her but her memory was a fog. She tried to move her hand only to find it bound. That realization cleared her head instantly.

She pulled at her hands, then at the binding on her feet. She was tied up. She struggled to sit up and look around. She was in a room that looked abandoned, like an old house that had been left in ruins. Junk was piled in one corner, rolls of carpet lay on the floor and garbage littered the room. She looked up and realized the ceiling was also falling down in places.

She struggled to recall what had happened and remembered her discovery about Ken and his grabbing her and drugging her. She also remembered he wasn't who he'd claimed to be. Ken Barrett was a fake identity he'd used to get close to her. He was actually the son of Kathryn Rollins.

She heard movement and realized it was birds flying through holes in the ceiling. Then she heard another faint sound that grabbed her attention—the sound of a child crying. She strained to listen closer and heard the soft sounds again. Realization pulsed through her. It was Jacob! She was certain that was his cry.

She pulled at the bonds, more determined than ever to get free. She had to reach her son. She finagled the ties around her hands. When she was finally free she saw they were red and raw. But the pain didn't matter nearly as much as reaching Jacob. She loosened the ties on her feet and tossed them aside then rushed out of the room, her gait unsteady, obviously from the drugs Ken had given her. She held onto the wall and pushed open a heavy wooden door.

They were inside an old hotel. The floors were missing in several places and the walls seemed to bow, looking like they might fall at any moment. On one side of the massive lobby was what used to be the check-in desk but there were now holes in the counter and graffiti covered everything that was still standing.

In the center of the room was a large staircase that she could tell had once been impressive and an obvious focal point of the hotel. It was easy to imagine the giant structure in its heyday and it briefly saddened her to see it in such ruin, but she had other more pressing concerns than worrying about the sad state of some old hotel. She had to find her son.

She screamed and nearly fell when a flock of birds fluttered around her then flew up to the ceiling. She grabbed the banister to steady herself, but the old structure creaked under the pressure of her weight so she regained her balance quickly. There were no doubt many critters making this place their home and probably more than a few squatters, as well, if Ken hadn't already cleared the hotel of them. As the sounds of the birds faded away, she heard the cry again coming from upstairs.

Jacob!

It had to be him.

She rushed up the stairs, the pain in her head a second thought. She used the rickety banister only when she needed to and prayed it didn't give out on her. The sound of crying grew louder as she reached the top. It echoed through the empty halls and she realized it was coming from even farther up. She followed the stairs up several more flights, chasing the sound of the cries she knew had to belong to Jacob.

On the eleventh floor, she rushed into the hallway and checked every room. Toward the end of the long hall she noticed a door that looked new and sturdy and definitely out of place. The sound grew louder as she neared it. Her heart nearly burst from her chest when she saw her son sitting on a blanket on the floor in the middle of the room. His face was red from crying and anger burned through her. Why had they left him to cry this way? And why wasn't someone watching him?

She rushed into the room and scooped him up in her arms, her heart soaring to have him close to her again and to know that he was safe. *Thank You, Lord*, her heart cried, even as tears of relief and happiness spilled from her eyes. Jacob put his arms around her neck and snuggled his face into her. She patted his back and smoothed his hair, her hands unable to get enough of him, just to feel him in her arms again.

"My, my, what a joyous family reunion."

Ashlynn froze when she heard the voice and the ice in it. She turned and saw Ken standing in the open doorway, his gun drawn and pointed at her. Behind him stood a petite, dark-haired woman she didn't recognize. Barbara, no doubt.

Ashlynn pulled Jacob even tighter against her and backed away from them. "There was never an FBI agent you wanted us to meet with, was there? You used that to lure us to the office. What do you want with us?" she demanded. "Why are you doing this?"

"You know why, Ashlynn."

"It's because I helped send your mother to jail? I was a child, Ken, and she beat me so badly I nearly died."

"I wish you had died then," he hissed. "Because of you, my mother died in prison. Because of you, I grew up without a mother." He motioned toward Jacob. "Now your son will know the same life."

Ashlynn gripped him even tighter. "Please don't hurt him. He's just an innocent child."

"So was I," Ken bellowed, then his voice softened. "I was only a teenager, but you took everything from me. I could have just killed you when I grabbed you in your office, but I wanted you to know why this was happening. I wanted you to understand that I, Paul Rollins, was the one who tore your family apart, just as you did mine."

He motioned at the woman behind him and she approached Ashlynn, reaching for Jacob.

Ashlynn backed way. "No, leave him alone! Don't you know what's happening?" she asked the woman. "He kidnapped my son and now he's going to kill me."

Barbara didn't reply but held out her arms for the child.

Ken was quick with the gun. "Either let her have the kid or I'll shoot him right here."

Ashlynn could see the serious threat in his face and knew it wasn't idle. He would kill Jacob. "What are you going to do with him?"

"I'm going to do the same thing to him that you did to me. He'll end up in foster care. Maybe he'll be one of the fortunate ones and end up with a good family." His lips formed a sly grin. "Or maybe he won't. I guess you'll never know." He held the gun up again and pointed it at her. "Now hand him over."

God, what should I do? Handing Jacob over to Ken was like giving away a part of herself, but she knew it was better than his killing them both. Jacob might have a chance to live and have a future, even if it was in foster care. Not all foster families were like the Rollins home.

But the truth was that she had little choice. If she had to choose between her child living or dying, she would choose life for him. She wiped tears from his big, green eyes then kissed his cheek. "Mommy loves you," she whispered just as Barbara grabbed him.

Jacob screamed as the woman pulled him from Ashlynn's arms. He started crying again and reaching for her, tears streaming down his face. Ashlynn struggled to keep back her own emotion but her heart was being ripped from her chest with every scream. She closed her eyes as the woman and Jacob disappeared out the door, but his cries for her continued to echo through the empty building.

She had no choice in this matter. This was being done without her control and she couldn't stop it. She couldn't protect Jacob from the future Ken had planned for him and she wasn't going to be able to stop Ken from murdering her right here in this hotel.

Garrett had told her that God didn't often intervene in man's sins, but he'd assured her He worked to fix the wrongs caused by evil men. She looked at Ken and knew she was looking into the face of evil. She prayed God could redeem whatever Ken did here today. He might kill her, but God would still be able to restore Jacob's life. She found herself praying for her son, praying that God would keep His eye on him and give him a better life than Ken had planned for him.

And Garrett. She hated to think what would happen to him when he discovered he'd been unable to save either her or Jacob. Would he draw back into himself as he'd done after the ambush? Would he spend his life seeking revenge or self-destruction? She hoped not. She prayed he would find a way to grieve, then move on. And maybe God would use him to find Jacob and bring Ken and his girlfriend to justice. Hopefully, he would continue searching and save Jacob from the life Ken had planned for him.

"What are you going to do to me?" she asked. She knew he planned to kill her. He'd tried many times already. He wouldn't forfeit this chance.

"Did you know the city plans to tear this building down? Well, they're not going to get the chance. There is going to be a terrible fire. When the fire department finds a body, if they do, they'll just think you're one of the squatters that calls this place home. Even if they eventually identify you, I'll be long gone with your son." He shrugged. "I had hoped Barbara could get me another syringe but she wasn't able to, so I guess I'll have to do this the hard way."

Fear rippled through her as he lunged at her. He raised his gun and slammed it hard against her head. Pain blinded her for a moment then everything faded away.

TEN

Josh pulled up and parked at the curb across the street from the Royal Hotel. Garrett had read about this place and knew the city was planning to level the one-hundred-year-old abandoned building. It had once been grand, but had now stood empty for over thirty years. With the broken windows and accumulated garbage, he could understand why city leaders considered it an eyesore.

As they got out of Josh's car and moved to the back of the vehicle, a truck pulled in behind them and Levi got out. He looked robust and healthy as he greeted them both, but Garrett still saw the wounded man he'd carried out of the line of fire and remembered the man he'd left behind.

"Are you sure you're up for this?" Garrett asked him.

Levi groaned and rolled his eyes, obviously weary of people asking him that question. "I'm fine." He batted his chest. "The neurologist gave me a clean bill of health." He reached for a protective vest from Josh's trunk and slipped it on. "Now, what are we looking at inside? Multiple shooters?"

Garrett sighed and put aside his concerns about Levi and concentrated instead on the matter at hand. Vince and the police would be arriving soon, but Garrett was glad his friends were here for backup, too, because he was going into that hotel to find his family with or without the backing of JPD.

"Probably. I know there was more than one person shooting at us that night at my house. I'm pretty sure I wounded someone. One of Ken's friends, Meeks, is still sitting in a jail cell and he didn't have a gunshot wound so I'm assuming Ken has more people helping him. He must have recruited some of his army buddies."

Levi grinned and patted his back. "And you've got your army buddies helping you. Fair is fair."

Josh handed them each a rifle. "We know he took Ashlynn, and we know he's in there. Ashlynn has to be in there, too, and probably her son, as well."

"Anything else I need to know?" Levi asked.

Garrett nodded. "I'm not coming out of there without my family."

Levi didn't flinch at his words, only checked his weapon and locked eyes with him, his gaze steady and determined. "Then let's go get them."

They walked across the street and entered the hotel one by one, Garrett leading. His gun was raised and his senses on alert as the bright light of the afternoon gave way to the shadowy illumination of the hotel. Some light filtered in from the windows and the holes in the walls and ceiling, but it was very little and what made it through left patches of darkness. He scanned the lobby, noting the garbage and graffiti and junk from outside had filtered in here. But he saw no people. His pulse was pounding as he stepped gingerly on the floors, sensing Josh and Levi behind him, mimicking his actions.

Josh moved to his right to check out the registration desk while Levi cleared the downstairs rooms. Each of them gave the all-clear signal so Garrett headed upstairs.

He was halfway up the staircase when he heard heavy footsteps approaching and the sound of people talking.

"Have the charges been set?" He recognized Ken's voice.

"Yes, we've placed them strategically around the hotel. They're ready to go."

"Good, then let's get out of here."

A group of men rounded the corner and saw him a split second before he could retreat or hide. Garrett counted five men in army fatigues. He raised his gun but the man in front was quicker. He pulled his weapon and began firing. One of his bullets grazed Garrett's shoulder and he tumbled backward, rolling down the staircase. He hit the bottom and heard the floor crack beneath him but it didn't give under his weight.

Josh and Levi took cover and fired back. Garrett scrambled to conceal himself, too, as the five men in camo descended the stairs, guns raised and ready to fight. They spread out as they reached the lobby. Garrett glanced up and spotted Ken behind them along with a dark-haired woman who was holding a child. He couldn't see the child's face but felt certain it was Jacob. He blew out a steadying breath, readying himself for the firefight. He wasn't leaving this hotel without Jacob and they weren't leaving with him.

The guy in front moved cautiously, scanning the lobby for movement. Garrett jumped out. He rushed at the man and tackled him, knocking the rifle from his hand. He didn't stay down long, however. The others turned to help him and were confronted by Josh and Levi and the shady room was suddenly filled with the flickering light of gunfire.

Garrett punched the man with everything he had but finally used the butt of his own gun to take him down. The guy slumped back to the floor and Garrett scanned the lobby for his next target. He saw it when he spotted Ken and the woman taking shelter behind the staircase.

He swooped up his gun and lunged at Ken, prepared to do whatever it took to get his son.

The woman crouched, clutching Jacob to her while Ken squatted like a snake ready to attack. He glanced behind Garrett obviously hoping for some assistance from his friends, but Garrett knew Josh and Levi had taken care of those men.

"They can't help you," Garrett told him. "Now put your hands in the air."

He saw Ken's mind working, trying to figure out what to do. He grabbed Jacob from the woman, shoving her to the floor in the process, pulled his gun from his holster and pressed it against Jacob's temple.

Garrett's chest clenched and all the air seemed to leave him. Jacob began to cry and squirm, but Ken tightened his hold on him.

"I will shoot him," he warned, and Garrett believed him. He was like a trapped animal that wasn't going to give up without a fight.

Now Garrett's mind played through the scenarios and he couldn't come up with one that could remove his son safely from Ken's arms.

God, please don't let him hurt Jacob.

He wet his lips, which had suddenly become very dry, and then pushed away a trickle of sweat on his brow. He couldn't comprehend that this man might snatch his son from him before he'd even had an opportunity to get to know him. The thought sent ripples of panic through him.

And Ken must have seen that fear in his eyes because he sneered and pressed the gun to Jacob's temple again. "That's right. Now I have the upper hand. Put your weapon down. All of you, put your weapons down or I'll shoot the kid."

Garrett lowered his rifle and nodded at Josh and Levi to do the same. He knelt, his eyes never leaving Ken's, and set his rifle on the floor.

"Good, good."

"It's going to be okay, Jacob. Everything is going to be fine." Garrett kept his voice calm and smooth, hoping to reassure the boy whose cheeks and lips were red from crying and whose face was wet with tears.

But Garrett's words seem to anger Ken. "Don't tell him that," he insisted. "Don't lie to the boy. It won't be okay. After my mamma was arrested, everyone told me not to worry because everything would be okay. Only it wasn't. She was murdered in prison, and it's all Ashlynn's fault for sending her there."

He wondered briefly if Ken held any ill will toward the others involved in sending his mother to prison, like Judge Warren who'd prosecuted her, but quickly realized he'd heaped all his bitterness and anger on Ashlynn's shoulders. He was set on his revenge and nothing was going to stop him. Garrett quickly surmised there would be no reasoning with him and no peaceful negotiations for the return of his son.

If Ken got out of the hotel with Jacob, the boy would be gone from them forever.

He reacted on instinct, sliding toward Ken like he was sliding into home plate. He kicked his legs out from under him and Ken fell. He heard the crack of the wood beneath Ken's feet and knew Josh and Levi were also on the move. But all his concentration was on Jacob, who rolled from Ken's arms as he fell and hit the floor. Garrett swooped him up and quickly put some distance between him and Ken.

But Ken wasn't giving up so easily. Garrett heard the click of a safety and knew Ken had retrieved the gun he'd dropped. He froze and turned back. Ken indeed had the gun pointed at them.

Garrett swallowed hard. His rifle was on the other side of the room and he had no way to protect them except by reaching the door. Ashlynn broke into his thoughts and he wondered if he would see her again.

Ken fired and the bullet flew past him, but he quickly raised the gun to fire again.

A second shot, this one fired from Levi's rifle, went right into the back of Ken's head. The man slumped, then hit the floor, the gun tumbling from his hand.

The woman screamed when he fell. She raised her hands above her head in surrender. Levi quickly bound her hands as he had the rest of Ken's men.

Garrett looked at Levi, gratitude rushing through him, and nodded as a way of thanks. He would have much more to say later when he was able to speak again, but for now it would have to do. Levi returned his nod then began helping Josh round up the men who'd helped Ken.

Garrett heard sirens outside and knew Vince and the police task force had finally arrived.

He carried his son outside as the police squad hurried past him into the building. He leaned against the building, taking a moment to relish the feel of Jacob's small frame in his arms. The boy was still crying, but was now clinging to Garrett, his face pressed into his shoulder.

Thank You, Lord, for this moment.

He carried Jacob to a police cruiser and opened the back door, placing the boy on the seat. He found a blanket and wrapped it around his shoulders then knelt before him and rubbed a hand over his fine sandy hair. "Are you okay, Jacob? Did that man hurt you?"

Jacob choked back sobs but shook his head *no* instead of answering. He looked small and frail, his big eyes wide with fear and his lashes wet. His chin quivered as he asked, "Where's my mommy?"

"She's going to be fine," Garrett assured him, rubbing his hand over the boy's hair again. He knew in an instant he could spend hours looking into this child's face and being mesmerized by his chubby cheeks and big, round eyes. This was his son, his child, and it would take months, maybe even years for him to wrap his head around that.

But he couldn't take that time right at the moment. He had to hand Jacob off to an officer to watch over him because five little words kept pulsating through his brain, words that could mean devastation for his and Jacob's future.

Have the charges been set?

Ken Barrett had planted bombs inside the Royal Hotel.

He ran back inside, fear igniting his steps. He had to get to Ashlynn. He had to find her. She hadn't come when she'd heard the gunfight which meant she was either tied up, unconscious, or...

He grimaced. He couldn't even go there.

He pushed back through the revolving doors and saw officers hovering over Ken's body. Josh and Levi were speaking with Vince and the other detectives, obviously unaware of the bombs. They must have been too far away to have heard Ken ask about the charges.

"There's a bomb in the building!" Garrett hollered and everyone's head popped up. "Ken asked his men if they'd set charges. That must mean there's a bomb in the building, or possibly several."

Josh motioned outside, toward the group of men who'd been Ken's accomplices. "That's why those guys were so eager to be taken out of here."

"Everyone out!" Vince shouted, waving his hands. "I'm calling the bomb squad."

Garrett headed for the stairs but Levi gripped his arm. "Where are you going?"

"Ashlynn is still missing and probably somewhere in this building. I can't leave her."

He nodded. "Then I'm coming with you."

"Me, too," Josh said.

Garrett didn't bother trying to talk them out of it. In truth, he was glad for their decision.

"I'm going to question those guys," Vince called to them. "Maybe they'll tell me exactly where they hid those bombs."

Garrett nodded then headed up the steps, wondering how much time they had. Had the bombs been on a timer? He hadn't seen one. If they'd been on a timer, there was no telling how many precious minutes they had before they detonated.

As he reached the stop of the stairs, he heard the boom of an explosion then the crack of wood as the ceiling above him collapsed.

Time was up.

Ashlynn coughed, smoke choking her as she regained consciousness. It was billowing in beneath the door. Dread filled her and she felt physically ill. Ken had started a fire…and he had Jacob. She crawled to her feet and stumbled toward the door but felt the heat of the fire outside through the wood. She grabbed a piece of cloth and tried to turn the doorknob.

Locked.

He'd locked her inside to die in the fire. She hadn't seen a room with a door anywhere in this hotel when she was searching for Jacob, but one look at the shiny new hinges and she knew Ken had hung it just for this purpose.

Without her cell phone, she had no way to call for help and her only way out was blocked. She hurried to the window and looked out. She was on a high floor, too high to jump, but she had no choice. Her only chance of surviving and getting Jacob back was getting out of this room. She would take everything else step by step.

Oh, Lord, please guide my steps. Keep my son safe. And please bring me through this safely.

She pulled at the window but it wouldn't open. In her fear, she wanted to break down and cry but that wouldn't do any good and it would only use up valuable time and energy. Ken had planned well. This was probably the only room in the entire hotel with a working door and glass in the window.

She coughed as the smoke started getting to her. How she wished Garrett was here. She should never have been so hard on him. She shouldn't have said those terrible things to him because she knew they weren't true. It had only been her own insecurities surfacing. She could trust him. Ironically, she knew that now when she couldn't even tell him. Was she going to die with him believing she never loved him?

Despite what she'd told him, she knew Garrett would come for her. Yes, he had let her down once before, but she realized she'd allowed that anger and bitterness to color her judgment. She'd wasted her life worrying about being hurt so much that she'd closed herself off to truly loving someone…and from allowing God to work in her life. In her heart, she knew Garrett wouldn't stop searching until he found her and that gave her comfort. The question was would he make it in time to save her? Or to save Jacob?

Anger ripped through her at the thought of all that Ken had taken from her. She thought of her son and of Ken carrying him out. Jacob had been crying for her and that riled her up even more. She needed that adrenaline kick. She picked up a piece of wood and rammed against the window this time calling on that extra boost of energy. The glass shattered.

She brushed away pieces of broken glass from the sill and stuck her head outside, taking in a big gulp of fresh air. She could see police cars with their flashing lights on the street below and hope filled her. They'd found her. They were coming for her. But when she looked down she realized the fire truck's ladder was extended but wasn't long enough to reach the floor she was on. She was on her own unless she could make it down a few flights of stairs.

Suddenly the door exploded behind her sending fragments of wood and metal into the room. She screamed and hit the floor, but a piece of something sharp sliced into her back. She cried out in pain and very nearly curled up to die.

But she didn't. The police cars were outside which meant they had found her. Garrett had to be down there and he would not let her die here in this hotel. He would come for her just as she'd known in her heart he would. She had to stay alive for him, for a second chance to tell him she loved him and to introduce him to his son. More than anything, she wanted to be a family with him.

She thought of how he'd told her that terrible things happened to people but that God was always with them. She believed him now. She felt God's presence here in the room with her, providing her comfort and reassurance that she wasn't alone.

That had been the worst part of her life, she realized. Not that unspeakable things had happened to her, but that she'd been forced to endure them alone. She'd never been surrounded by people who loved her enough to stand beside her during times of distress. She realized now she hadn't needed anyone besides Jesus. He'd always been there for her and with her, whispering His love to her and asking for her trust. He didn't hate her. He'd loved her so much that He'd died for her on the cross.

And suddenly she knew He was someone she could absolutely trust with all her heart. She was going to get through this because of Him.

She edged nearer the window again, wincing against the heat of the fire that was now pressing into the room. She climbed through the window, shards of hot glass digging into her hands and knees. She dangled her foot until she felt something solid beneath her then carefully stood and moved along the ledge, pressing herself against the building for support. She was afraid to look down, afraid of losing her balance and falling or just being paralyzed with fear. But she wasn't giving up. She needed to reach another room where the fire wasn't raging so badly. If she could get there and make it down to a lower floor then the fire department could reach her. It was her only chance of surviving this.

Guide my steps, oh Lord. Guide my steps.

She inched along the ledge until she came to the next window. This one had no glass, but one peek inside told her she had to keep going. The flames were already inside this room and swiping at the walls. She moved back the other way but the same thing was happening in the window of the room she'd just left. She was trapped. She couldn't go back inside and she couldn't move past either window. She was stuck on this ledge on the eleventh floor of the Royal Hotel.

She only thought things couldn't get any worse until she heard a loud noise and looked down at her feet.

The ledge beneath her was cracking.

Levi grabbed Garrett's collar and pulled him backward as a chunk of ceiling nearly fell on top of him.

He started digging through the wreckage, trying to clear a path, but Josh grabbed his arm. "We can't make it up that way."

"I have to get to her," Garrett insisted, fear and adrenaline propelling him.

"It's too heavy," Levi insisted. "The staircase is about to collapse."

As if in response, the wood of the staircase creaked and gave way, sending all three of them falling. A thick coat of debris landed on top of them, threatening to bury them again. Garrett gathered his senses as quickly as he could and crawled out of the rubble. The staircase was no longer connected to the floor above them. The head of it lay in a heap on the lobby floor. It was gone along with his best chance of reaching Ashlynn.

Coughing brought him back to the situation. Levi pushed aside several pieces of rubble and climbed to his feet. Josh did the same. They both appeared to be unhurt.

"We have to find a way up there," Garrett told them. "I can shimmy up a rope to reach the next floor."

"This whole building is about to collapse," Josh said. "If you try to anchor a rope up there, you'll bring the whole second floor down on top of you." He coughed and looked around at the garbage surrounding them. "What's left of it, anyway."

He shook his head, waving off their concerns. "I have to try."

"It's too dangerous," Josh hollered, then both he and Levi took one of Garrett's arms and pulled him towards the exit.

"I can't leave her," Garrett insisted, struggling to break their holds.

"We'll find another way," Levi said. "This isn't over."

But all Garret could see was the image of Marcus's body as Garrett left him. He wouldn't leave Ashlynn behind as he had Marcus. He wouldn't!

They dragged him outside and Garrett saw the men who'd been working with Ken. He hurried over and confronted one, pulling on his shirt. "Where's Ashlynn? What did Ken do with her?"

The man shook his head. "I don't know," he said, but his tone implied that he did know but didn't care to share it.

"Where is she?" Garrett screamed, seriously on the verge of losing control of himself. He was glad Josh and Levi were there to pull him back.

"Mama!" Jacob cried, his scream carrying over the sound of the sirens and the fire hoses.

Garrett had heard the boy's shrieks ever since leaving the hotel, but this one, this cry for his mother, sounded different. He glanced at Jacob, who was squirming in an officer's arms and reaching out, pointing back up at the hotel.

Garrett turned to look and felt his blood go cold when he saw a figure move on one of the top floors where the fire was raging. But she wasn't inside the hotel. She was outside on the ledge and fire was bursting through the open windows around her.

"Ashlynn!"

He was about to bolt back into the building when several hands stopped him.

"You can't go in there," Josh told him. His face was covered in dirt, but his expression was firm.

"I have to. Ashlynn is up there."

"We'll find another way," Levi said. He, too, was covered in dust, but his eyes were locked on Garrett's determinedly. "We're not giving up on her, but you can't get up to that floor that way. We've already tried, remember?"

Garrett nodded his understanding. He heard them. He knew what they were saying was right, but he had to get to her. He couldn't stand here doing nothing and watch her die. Their hands didn't move from his arms until he relented and turned back. He raked his hands over his face. There had to be a way to reach her. *Oh, God, please help me save her.*

He lifted his eyes upward. He wasn't alone, but he knew he needed more help than the rangers or even the police could give him on this one. He needed God's guidance. He lifted his eyes upward and noticed a cross atop the building beside the Royal. It was lit up bright with Christmas lights. That's what he needed to see—something to help his mind focus. He wouldn't hear God's wisdom if he allowed panic and fear to guide him. He closed his eyes and tried to clear his mind, concentrating only on the image of the cross. But when he opened his eyes again, he saw something else.

The building with the cross matched the Royal in height and the side facing the old hotel had windows. If he could get inside that building, up to that floor, he could crawl across to where Ashlynn was trapped on that ledge.

"I need rope," he said, causing both Josh and Levi to look up. He knew Josh was going to remind him that roping up wouldn't be possible, but before he spoke, he followed Garrett's gaze and instantly seemed to reach the same conclusion.

"I have a grappling rope in my truck," Levi said and took off running to retrieve it.

Garrett ran to the building with the cross and up the front stairs, only to find the doors locked tight.

"I'll have the police call the building manager," Josh said, but Garrett shook his head.

"No time." He pulled his gun and fired several shots at the locks, then kicked the door open, causing an alarm to sound. The gunfire also caused a roar among the street full of police behind him. He ignored it all and headed for the stairs. The alarm could barely be heard over the police and sirens and roar of the fire next door. He would gladly pay for the door he'd busted and any other damage he did, but he had to reach that top floor.

He heard Josh's footsteps on the stairs with him as he climbed and finally burst through the stairwell door and into one of the offices with windows facing the Royal. He pushed open the window and leaned out. "I'm coming to get you, Ashlynn," he called out to her.

She must have heard his voice over the roar because she looked his way. Relief flowed over her when she spotted him, momentarily drowning out the fear in her expression.

"Hang on. I'm coming."

She nodded her understanding but remained pressed against the building. She was breathing heavily and he knew she was frightened, but he saw something else in her face now. Hope.

Levi appeared moments later carrying his grappling ropes and launcher. Garrett was glad he had those.

He'd thought he might have to improvise something that wouldn't be as safe.

"Try to get it close to her," Garrett instructed as Levi loaded up the grappling gun. He half expected Levi to give him that *duh* look because it was so obvious a direction, but he didn't. Garrett pointed to a window only a few feet from where Ashlynn stood on the ledge. "See if you can hit that window right there."

He took aim then stopped and looked at Garrett. "This won't be very stable. The building is compromised, so don't take your time."

"Understood," Garrett said.

Levi took aim again and shot. The grappling hook hit the empty window sill then bounced off, not connecting. Levi unlatched the rope and it wound back up. He reinserted the hook and fired again. This time, it connected with the open window about a foot from Ashlynn.

"Got it!" he shouted. He pulled on the rope to make sure it was secure and nodded at Garrett.

Garrett felt his fear turn to steady determination. He couldn't think about the consequences. All he knew was that he had to reach her. He allowed Josh and Levi to secure the ropes around him.

"They're fine," he barked, as they double-checked them, knowing it was only his agitation at work.

Josh tightened them. "They're not fine. This rope could be the only thing that keeps you both from plummeting to the street below."

Garrett stared at Ashlynn out on that ledge and the

fear in her face was nearly more than he could stand. "I have to get to her."

"The rope isn't stable," Levi told him. "I can't guarantee it will hold with the building crumbling around it." He wasn't saying it in a way to try to talk Garrett out of going because he was sure Levi knew nothing was going to change his mind, but rather just for clarification.

Josh touched his shoulder. "We'll be praying for you," he said before tapping Garrett's shoulder in a way that meant he was good to go.

Garrett whispered a prayer of his own then released the lever and zipped across the expanse separating the two buildings. He grazed the crumbling ledge of the Royal then kicked his feet until he felt the landing. He spotted Ashlynn, still frozen in fear, and shouted to her over the roar of the fire and the noise.

"Ashlynn, come toward me!" She was still a good distance away from him and the fire that raged inside was still blocking her path, but she nodded and took a deep steadying breath before she started moving his way, inching along at a snail's pace. He watched her, the horrible feeling of being unable to do anything to help soaring through him. He didn't dare try to hurry her. If she fell, that would be the end. He reached out his arm for her, coaxing her along like a child learning to walk.

"Come on, baby. You can do it."

Fear shone in her eyes but she locked her gaze with his, nodded and kept moving, her hands pressed against the building and her feet sliding along the ledge. The heat of the stone she was clinging to had to be unbearably hot against her skin, but she didn't show it.

He held his breath. She was only a few inches from him now, nearly close enough that he could reach out and grab her. He stretched his arms, pulling the expanse of his gear to the edge of functionality. She reached out her hand for his and he coaxed her along.

"You've got this, baby. You're nearly there."

He saw her face change a second before the ledge cracked beneath her feet. "Garrett!" she screamed as it gave way and crumbled, sending her falling.

Something hard grabbed her, stopping her in midair. She looked up and saw Garrett's hand firmly around her arm. Her other arm was dangling along with her feet, and she was certain she heard a collective gasp from the crowd below.

Every muscle in his shoulder and arm seemed to tense and his face grimaced in pain, but he pulled her up slowly.

"Hang on, Ashlynn. I've got you. I'm not letting you go." His voice was clipped, but the determination on his face was very real.

His jaw tensed as his hand slipped on her skin. She felt his grip giving way and saw a spot of what looked like blood on his sleeve brighten and get bigger. His shoulder had been injured yet he was still holding on to her with all his might.

That was love.

He tightened his grip and took a deep breath then hauled her quickly toward him.

She used her other hand to grab hold of his vest.

"Pull yourself up, baby," he said and she did.

Finally she clutched his shoulders and wrapped both arms around his neck. His body relaxed, but his non-injured arm tightened around her.

"I've got you," he whispered, breathing hard. "I'm not letting you go again."

Fear rippled through her, along with relief and gratitude, but they weren't out of danger yet. They were still hanging on a rope in the air far from the street below and she wasn't yet convinced they were out of danger.

But she wasn't alone. Garrett had come for her just as she'd known he would.

He tied the rope around her and secured it to the pulley. But it was useless a moment later when fire burst through the windows and the structure began to creak. Ashlynn noticed his friends motioning for them to hurry. She could bask in her thankfulness once they were safely away from the Royal Hotel.

He pushed off the building, but the rope above them went slack as the top of the hotel began to crumble.

"Hold on!" he shouted to Ashlynn as their lifeline gave way and sent them falling. She burrowed her head into his shoulder and held on tight as they swung toward the other building.

They hit the side of the building hard. Garrett took the brunt of the force with his back and she doubted that was by accident. He'd steered them so he would be the one to sustain the hit, and she could see from the way his face paled that it hurt. It hurt her, too, causing her breath to leave her for a moment as pain riddled her body. She lost her grip on him and nearly slipped away, but Garrett pulled her tighter against him.

He used the building as leverage, swinging outward then back to the building, this time aiming for a window near where they'd landed before. He had to hit it twice before it shattered and he could grab hold of the ledge. She saw blood and knew he'd cut his hands on the glass. But he steadied them and carefully unhooked her from the rope.

She climbed through the window and was nearly bent over with relief to be back on solid ground. Garrett followed and she glanced up at him. He looked bloody and tired, but his eyes shone with happiness.

She threw herself into his arms and he swept her up in them, claiming her lips with his, as relief and elation flowed through her with so much joy she thought it would overwhelm her. She'd never been so grateful in her life and so thankful that God had brought them to safety.

But she realized it wasn't over. She suddenly pushed away from him as thoughts of her son rushed through her. "Jacob!"

He pressed a finger to her lips to quiet her. "He's safe," Garrett quickly reassured her. "We caught Ken leaving the hotel. He's dead and all those working with him are in custody. Jacob is fine."

She relaxed and leaned into him, realizing she'd been wrong before. Now, she'd never been so grateful. Her child was safe, her tormentor dead and the danger to them gone. She looked up into Garrett's wide, green eyes and felt herself finally, blissfully relax.

Tears pooled in her eyes and she didn't bother trying to stop them. "I knew you would come for me," she whispered to him. "I knew you wouldn't let me down."

He pressed his forehead to hers. "I'm never leaving you again," he said, his voice low and gruff with emotion. "Never."

She gave a small sigh of relief as she settled into his embrace and he closed his arms around her. "I believe you."

She heard heavy footsteps approaching and shouts. Garrett glanced towards them. "That's just Josh and Levi coming to make sure we're okay." He shrugged. "Let them wait." He took her face in his hands and kissed her long and hard.

EPILOGUE

Ashlynn parked her car in the garage and entered her house, noting how quiet it seemed. Fear darted through her for a moment, reminding her of the day she'd returned home to find Mira dead and Jacob gone, but that fear quickly dissipated when she walked toward the back door and heard Jacob's squeal of delight coming from the backyard.

She pushed open the sliding doors and smiled when she saw what was happening. Garrett had Jacob across his arms and was spinning around, flying him like an airplane. Jacob was loving every minute of it.

"Faster, Daddy," Jacob hollered, causing Ashlynn's heart to fill again at her son's use of the name.

She smiled at their antics. It had taken a while for Jacob to warm up to Garrett, but Ashlynn's encouragement had helped the boy along. Jacob had been through a lot in the past few months. He missed Stephen, who he called his first daddy, and missed the way Mira made him PB and J sandwiches. And he still occasionally awoke screaming in fear that the bad men were going to come get him again. But the therapist she'd taken him to had assured her that the nightmare would eventually fade for him now that he once again had a stable home environment.

It pained her to think of all the time Garrett had spent alone when he'd had a family here. He should have been with them from the start and while she still didn't understand why God had allowed them to be separated for all those years, she was thankful He'd brought Garrett back to them.

"Mommy's home," Jacob cried, and Garrett set him down, whispering something into his ear and sliding something into his hand.

Jacob ran to her. "Mama, Mama, I got this for you," he said in his sweet little voice.

"What is it, baby?" She held out her hand and he placed something in it. She expected another flower picked from the grass or a slimy frog he'd found hopping around, but the object he placed in her hand was small and round and shiny. It was a ring…an engagement ring.

She glanced up at Garrett, who was grinning big and broad.

"What is this?" she asked, her breath on hold as her heart skipped a beat.

He pulled her to her feet, grasping her hands in his. "I love you, Ashlynn, and when I was away from you and Jacob my life didn't have any meaning. I was an empty shell of a man. You brought me back to life. You and Jacob gave me back the one thing I thought I'd lost, a reason for living. I don't ever want to be without you again. Will you be my wife?"

She couldn't have stopped the waves of giddy laughter that erupted in her even if she'd wanted to. Her heart swelled and tears pooled in her eyes. "Nothing on this Earth would make me happier than becoming your wife, Garrett."

"Mama, why you crying?" Jacob asked.

She scooped him up and hugged him. "Because I'm happy, baby. I'm so very happy."

Garrett slid the ring onto her finger, then leaned in and kissed her.

She had her son back and the man she loved with her. Most of all, she had the family she'd always dreamed of having.

God had truly blessed her with everything she'd ever wanted.

* * * * *

If you liked this story, pick up these other
RANGERS UNDER FIRE *books*
by Virginia Vaughan:

YULETIDE ABDUCTION
REUNION MISSION
RANCH REFUGE

Available now from Love Inspired!

Find more great reads at www.LoveInspired.com.

Dear Reader,

Thanks so much for reading Garrett and Ashlynn's story!

Have you ever felt like God just wasn't on your side? Sure you have. We all know that feeling. Life is hard and in some seasons of our lives we get beaten up by circumstances. It is so easy to forget that God is present and active in our lives. This is how Ashlynn feels at the beginning of the story. Everything she has fought so hard for all her life has been ripped away from her, and she is so angry and bitter at God that she cannot imagine putting her trust in Him. But Garrett's reappearance in her life at just the time she needs him helps show Ashlynn that God, indeed, is with her and that He works all things for good.

In Deuteronomy 2:15 God assured Moses and the Israelites that He had been with them throughout their forty years of wandering in the desert. We have the same assurance that God is with us, watching over us and providing for us.

I love hearing from readers. You can connect with me through my website, www.virginiavaughanonline.com, or through the publisher.
Blessings!

Virginia

COMING NEXT MONTH FROM
Love Inspired® Suspense

Available January 3, 2017

BIG SKY SHOWDOWN • by Sharon Dunn
As Zane Scofield guides Heather Jacobs through the mountains of Montana to fulfill her father's dying wish, someone from Zane's shadowy past attacks them. Now they must find a way to stop a gang of criminals...and survive a treacherous chase through the mountains.

UNDERCOVER PROTECTOR
Wilderness, Inc. • by Elizabeth Goddard
Hoping to bring down the person in charge of a wildlife trafficking ring, Special Agent Grayson Wilde goes undercover at Gemma Rollins's tiger sanctuary. At first, he's convinced Gemma must be involved, but when someone tries to kill her, all that matters is keeping her alive.

MOUNTAIN AMBUSH
Echo Mountain • by Hope White
A search-and-rescue mission turns deadly when Dr. Kyle Spencer is nearly killed by a masked assailant in the mountains. EMT Maddie McBride saves the doctor just in time—but now they're both targets for murder.

BURIED MEMORIES • by Carol J. Post
As the mysterious threats on her life escalate, Nicki Jackson wonders if her nightmares of a murder are actually hidden memories. Childhood friend ex-soldier Tyler Brant vows to protect Nicki while she sorts out her past—even if it puts his own life in danger.

DEAD RUN • by Jodie Bailey
When Kristin James is attacked while out for a run, she assumes it's a crime of convenience...until the culprit mentions her brother, who died in combat. Staff Sergeant Lucas Murphy rescues her, but she'll never be safe—unless they uncover her brother's secrets.

CONCEALED IDENTITY • by Jessica R. Patch
After DEA agent Holt McKnight's criminal informant disappears, Holt must go undercover to get close to Blair Sullivan—the missing man's sister, who may know more than she's letting on. And when she's targeted by the drug cartel Holt's trying to take down, only he can save her.

REQUEST YOUR FREE BOOKS!
2 FREE RIVETING INSPIRATIONAL NOVELS
PLUS 2 FREE MYSTERY GIFTS

Love Inspired.
SUSPENSE
RIVETING INSPIRATIONAL ROMANCE

YES! Please send me 2 FREE Love Inspired® Suspense novels and my 2 FREE mystery gifts (gifts are worth about $10). After receiving them, if I don't wish to receive any more books, I can return the shipping statement marked "cancel." If I don't cancel, I will receive 4 brand-new novels every month and be billed just $4.99 per book in the U.S. or $5.49 per book in Canada. That's a savings of at least 17% off the cover price. It's quite a bargain! Shipping and handling is just 50¢ per book in the U.S. and 75¢ per book in Canada.* I understand that accepting the 2 free books and gifts places me under no obligation to buy anything. I can always return a shipment and cancel at any time. Even if I never buy another book, the two free books and gifts are mine to keep forever.

123/323 IDN GH5Z

Name _____ (PLEASE PRINT) _____

Address _____ Apt. # _____

City _____ State/Prov. _____ Zip/Postal Code _____

Signature (if under 18, a parent or guardian must sign) _____

Mail to the **Reader Service:**
IN U.S.A.: P.O. Box 1867, Buffalo, NY 14240-1867
IN CANADA: P.O. Box 609, Fort Erie, Ontario L2A 5X3

**Are you a current subscriber to Love Inspired® Suspense books
and want to receive the larger-print edition?
Call 1-800-873-8635 or visit www.ReaderService.com.**

* Terms and prices subject to change without notice. Prices do not include applicable taxes. Sales tax applicable in N.Y. Canadian residents will be charged applicable taxes. Offer not valid in Quebec. This offer is limited to one order per household. Not valid for current subscribers to Love Inspired Suspense books. All orders subject to credit approval. Credit or debit balances in a customer's account(s) may be offset by any other outstanding balance owed by or to the customer. Please allow 4 to 6 weeks for delivery. Offer available while quantities last.

Your Privacy—The Reader Service is committed to protecting your privacy. Our Privacy Policy is available online at www.ReaderService.com or upon request from the Reader Service.
We make a portion of our mailing list available to reputable third parties that offer products we believe may interest you. If you prefer that we not exchange your name with third parties, or if you wish to clarify or modify your communication preferences, please visit us at www.ReaderService.com/consumerschoice or write to us at Reader Service Preference Service, P.O. Box 9062, Buffalo, NY 14240-9062. Include your complete name and address.

SPECIAL EXCERPT FROM

SUSPENSE

When an ordinary trip into the Montana mountains leads to a deadly game of cat and mouse, can wilderness expert Zane Scofield protect himself and Heather Jacobs...or will his dangerous past doom them both?

Read on for a sneak preview of
BIG SKY SHOWDOWN
by Sharon Dunn, available January 2017 from Love Inspired Suspense!

Zane Scofield stared through his high-powered binoculars, scanning the hills and mountains all around him. For the last day or so, he'd had the strange sense that they were being watched. Who had been stalking them and why?

He saw movement through his binoculars and focused in. Several ATVs were headed down the mountain toward the campsite where he'd left Heather alone. He zeroed in and saw the handmade flag. He knew that flag. His mind was sucked back in time seven years ago to when he had lived in these mountains as a scared seventeen-year-old. If this was who he thought it was, Heather was in danger.

He could hear the ATVs drawing closer, but not coming directly into the camp. They were headed a little deeper into the forest. He ran toward the mechanical sound, pushing past the rising fear.

He called for Heather only once. He stopped to listen.

He heard her call back—faint and far away, repeating his name. He ran in the direction of the sound with his rifle still slung over his shoulder. When he came to the clearing, he saw a boy not yet in his teens throwing rocks into a hole and screaming, "Shut up. Be quiet."

Zane held his rifle up toward the boy. He could never shoot a child, but maybe the threat would be enough.

The kid grew wide-eyed and snarled at him. "More men are coming. So there." Then the boy darted into the forest, yelling behind him, "You won't get away."

Zane ran over to the hole. Heather gazed up at him, relief spreading across her face.

Voices now drifted through the trees, men on foot headed this way.

Zane grabbed an evergreen bough and stuck it in the hole for Heather to grip. She climbed agilely and quickly. He grabbed her hand and pulled her the rest of the way out. "We have to get out of here."

There was no time to explain the full situation to her. His worst nightmare coming true, his past reaching out to pull him into a deep dark hole. The past he thought he'd escaped.

If Willis was back in the high country, he needed to get Heather to safety and fast. He knew what Willis was capable of. Their lives depended on getting out of the high country.

Don't miss
BIG SKY SHOWDOWN
by Sharon Dunn, available wherever
Love Inspired® Suspense books and ebooks are sold.

www.LoveInspired.com

LISEXP1216

As Nick settled behind the steering wheel and started his truck, he slanted a look at Darcy. "So what do you think about the boys ranch?"

"Corey is much better off here than with his dad. He's not happy right now, but then he wasn't happy at home."

"He's scared." That was why Bea had brought him to the barn first to see Nick. "He'll feel better after he meets some of the other boys his age."

"What if he doesn't?" Darcy asked.

"He's confused. He wants to be with his dad, and yet not if he's always being left alone. He doesn't know what to expect from day to day and certainly doesn't feel safe." Those same feelings used to plague Nick while he was growing up.

"I've dealt with kids like that."

"In a perfect world, Ned wouldn't drink and would love Corey unconditionally. But that isn't going to happen. Ned isn't going to change." He knew firsthand the mind-set of an alcoholic and remembered the times his dad promised to stop drinking and reform. He never did; in fact he got worse.

"How do you know that for sure?"

"I just do." He didn't share his past with anyone. It was a part of his life he wanted to wipe from his mind, but it was always there in the background. He never wanted to see a child grow up the way he had.

"Then I'll pray for the best for Corey," Darcy said.

"The best scenario would be the state taking Corey away from Ned and a good family adopting him. I wish I was in a position to do it." The second he said that last sentence he wanted to snatch it back. He had no business being anyone's father.

"Because you're single? That might not matter in certain cases."

"I'm not dad material." How could he explain that he was struggling to erase the debt that his father had accumulated? If he lost the ranch, he would lose his home and job. But, more important, what if he wasn't a good father to Corey? It was one thing to be there to help when needed, but it was very different to be totally responsible for raising a child.

Don't miss
THE COWBOY'S TEXAS FAMILY
by Margaret Daley, available January 2017 wherever
Love Inspired® books and ebooks are sold.

www.LoveInspired.com

Love the Love Inspired book you just read?

Your opinion matters.

Review this book on your favorite book site, review site, blog or your own social media properties and share your opinion with other readers!

Be sure to connect with us at:
Harlequin.com/Newsletters
Twitter.com/LoveInspiredBks
Facebook.com/LoveInspiredBooks